AF595603

SMUGGLERS, GANGSTERS, AND AN ALLOSAURUS

SMUGGLERS, GANGSTERS, AND AN
ALLOSAURUS

PAUL V. CWIAKALA

Silk Baron Independent Press
Fair Lawn, New Jersey

Published in the United States by Silk Baron Independent Press.
First Edition: May 2022

Cover design by Silk Baron Independent Press
Book design and production by Silk Baron Independent Press
Editing by Silk Baron Independent Press

Silk Baron Independent Press
www.silkbaronindependentpress.com

To Uncle Ralph,
Thank you for listening, being there,
and all the years of love.

Table of Contents

The Monster at Arden Point

Arden Point was a small beach a few miles south of a town called Steinhatchee, an out of the way spot on the Floridian Gulf Coast. Victoria's Buick sedan wasn't exactly suited for the rough dirt roads, muddy after the last thunderstorm, and she quickly regretted not taking Colin's advice to take the department's Landrover. Between the mud, the overgrowth, and a particularly stubborn gator who paid no heed to her horn as it meandered it's way across the road, it was a miracle she was running only half an hour late.

Victoria was just getting out of her eleven o'clock when Colin Pfieffer ambushed her that morning outside Walker Hall.

"Can you do me a favor?"

Colin had a falsetto voice with a singsong tone, a feature that grated on some. He wore a pink button-up and a brown leather vest, unbuttoned, with his usual thick-rimmed coke bottle glasses and faux-John Lennon hairstyle that was popular with the students and young professors. Victoria had smiled and sighed - she knew she'd say yes before he even asked the question.

"Department got a call a little while ago," he'd said. "The sheriff's department. Something about a sea serpent on the beach."

Victoria had rolled her eyes.

"Dean asked me to go, but I've got an appointment I can't cancel," Colin said. "Can you...?

"You know I can," Victoria said. Colin laughed, then fished a slip of paper from his typewriter bag.

"Here's the details," he said. "You'll want to give them a call first to find out exactly where. Probably just a rotting basking shark or whale guts."

Victoria glanced at the scribble before stuffing it into a back pocket.

"Or it could be..."

Colin laughed again. "In your dreams!

The beach itself was nothing unusual, besides the army of police milling about. A wooden blockade had been set up just where the road gave way to the beach, a sign with the message "POLICE ACTIVITY, DO NOT ENTER" nailed onto the front. She parked in front of it, grabbed her messenger bag and clamshell case, and stepped out.

"You from the maritime college?" Sheriff Watley matched the description the deputy had provided on the phone: gruff, portly, and an uncanny likeness to Richard Nixon - if the president were about fifty pounds overweight, that is.

He wore a wide-brimmed hat with the department logo emblazoned on it, and approached Victoria with a wannabe John Wayne strut. His drawl was more suggestive of Georgia than Gainesville.

"Sorry I'm late," Victoria said, offering her hand. Watley's face was stone, he didn't even glance at it.

"I thought you people were sending some professor," he said. "Culberson or something."

"We did," Victoria said, letting her hand fall back and doing her best to not roll her eyes. "I'm Dr. Culberson."

Watley muttered something under his breath and shook his head. Victoria pretended not to notice.

"It's over this way," Watley said. He lead Victoria toward the beach, toward a spot a mile further north where she could see another group of police officers had gathered.

"How long has it been here?" she said. "On the phone your deputy said-"

"A day," Watley said. "No more than that based on the rot. A couple of surfers found it this morning, though based on the beer cans scattered around some kids must've found it some time earlier and not bothered to report it. Gave those idiot hippies a hell of a fright I'm told. They're damned lucky the deputy decided to even check it out. We're not in the business of entertaining tall tales about sea monsters, miss. We're serious people down here, I run a tight department. If it were me, I'd have tossed them out for wasting our time with obvious nonsense. Maybe locked 'em up, I bet they were high anyway. But..."

The air around the corpse was sour, salty, and thick with flies. The Sheriff was probably right about the how long it had been there, but the moment Victoria set her eyes on it she couldn't help but grin. It was twenty feet long, give or take a foot, and in otherwise remarkably good condition. It had the tell-tale long neck and the serpent-like tail that led to so many "sea serpent" tales, two large front flippers (though the right flipper had a large chunk bitten off), and a small dorsal hump in the center of the shoulder blades. The skin was a blue-gray, grayer now in death, seasoned with dark brown spots speckled along the back of the neck and torso. It had a head reminiscent of a furless and earless dog - a pentagonal black nose, white whiskers, big brown eyes that had glassed over, a thick pink tongue lolling from its long still mouth.

"You know what it is?" Watley said. He sounded skeptical.

"I knew it," Victoria said, having never really heard his question. "A Spotted Whale Seal."

"A spotted whatsit?" Watley said. Victoria ignored him and quickly got to work, opening her clamshell case to retrieve a camera. She double-checked that film was loaded, screwed in a bulb into the flash, and snapped a picture.

"It's a kind of seal," Victoria said. "You know, the things at the circus that balance balls on their noses."

Watley made a grunting noise that Victoria guessed was supposed to be a laugh.

"I know what a seal is," he said. "That ain't no seal.

That's a goddamned lizard or sea serpent."

Victoria walked around to the other side and snapped another photo.

"No, Sheriff, I assure you it's not," Victoria said. She returned to her clamshell case to retrieve some bottles and other testing equipment. "A lot of people have thought that over the years, so you're not the first to make that mistake."

"How come I've never heard of this?" he said, following her a foot more closely than she was comfortable with.

"They're rare, for one thing," she said. "There's been maybe a handful of confirmed sightings in the last hundred years. We didn't even think they were real until around forty years ago when a Dutch freighter accidentally killed one near the Aleutians."

Watley grunted again. Victoria wondered if he'd been a hog in a past life. She cut several chunks of flesh from the corpse and, with tweezers, carefully slipped them into sample bottles.

"So you're saying sea serpents are real after all?" he said. Victoria sighed. He had a look on his face like a small child wrestling with the concept of elephants.

"Sea serpents and sea monsters are what happens when people who don't know what they're seeing try to explain it to others," she said. "Whale seals, giant squid, and giant oarfish are what they really saw."

Victoria placed the samples back in the clamshell case and rummaged through in search of a syringe.

"The real question is, what is it doing here?" she said. "Spotted Whale Seals are native to the Arctic. There's never before been a sighting in the Gulf."

Watley scratched his chin.

"I'd have thought the real question would be, 'what killed it?'"

Victoria looked up at him. He gestured back at the corpse - sure enough, there was a large bite wound at the base of the neck. How had she missed that?

"Any idea what could have done that?" he said. "That's one huge bite, bigger than any shark bite I've ever seen."

Victoria traced it with a finger.

"It's not a shark," she said. "The pattern's wrong."

"If I didn't know better," Watley said. "I'd say it looks like-"

"SHERIFF!"

Victoria and Watley turned to where the deputy pointed, just in time to see the biggest saltwater crocodile she'd ever seen blast out of the surf and sprint toward them. The group scattered in all directions.

"Christ!" Watley wheezed. The croc hissed in reply, its immense jaws open wide. It positioned itself between the police officers and the whale seal, establishing its claim over the carcass. Too stunned to do more than watch, the officers and Victoria just stared as the crocodile clamped its jaws around the seal's neck with a sickening crunch and, with surprising speed, dragged it back into the Gulf.

In the space of two minutes, both had vanished beneath the waves and the beach was still once again.

"Sheriff," Victoria said at last. "I think you've got an exotic animal smuggling problem."

Watley grunted.

Smugglers, Gangsters, and an Allosaurus

"You've never heard of Maple White Land?"

The man at the bar had already had two or three too many by the shine in his emerald eyes and the stink of Jack Daniels on his breath. The question was incredulous, as if Alvorado had claimed to have never heard of Australia or the Moon.

"You gotta be joking!" His jowls flapped like rubber as he chuckled. "Seriously? Hey, Billy-" The bartender, a freckled ginger with a crooked nose and poorly knotted tie, looked up from the beer mug he'd been cleaning. "-Get a load of this! Fella says he's never heard of Maple White Land."

The bartender smiled - he found it amusing too, though clearly not so riotously funny as his drunken patron.

"Next," the drunk said, finishing his whiskey and waving for another. "You'll tell me you've never heard of dinosaurs either!"

Alvorado rolled his eyes and took a sip of his beer, some American lager he'd not bothered to remember the name of.

"Of course I have," he said. "The big lizards from a million years ago."

That really got the drunk laughing. Alvorado shook his head as the man got up and wandered, wobbly, toward the restroom. The bartender, shaking his head but still smiling, walked over and topped off Alvorado's beer.

"You'll have to forgive him, he gets a bit chatty once he's gotten a few in him," the bartender said.

"What's he rambling about anyway?" Alvorado sipped his beer. It tasted both too hoppy and too watery for his liking.

"Some place in South America where the last dinosaurs live," the bartender said. "Some guy named White died finding it, around 50 years ago or so. It's pretty famous, actually, I'm surprised you've not heard of it."

Alvorado just shrugged his shoulders.

"Doesn't ring a bell," he lied.

It was after 9 P.M. when Alvorado left the bar, some local dive around the block from his hotel in Miami Beach. Half-dressed twenty-somethings, some already drunk and smelling of reefer, clogged the streets as they danced and sang the chorus to Bob Dylan's newest single. None paid him more than a glance as he returned to the hotel and called for a cab to the Port of Miami.

Alvorado was no stranger to Miami, having managed nearly a dozen shipments since taking over for Ruiz after his accident. And since Castro took over, the American clientele seemed to almost entirely relocate to Florida. Sensible, as this was probably the closest the United States got to the appropriate climate. The animals had been very popular attractions for the hotels in Havana, he understood, and the Americans were clearly eager for more.

The S.S. Wanderer had arrived right on schedule and was already docked by the time Alvorado's taxi pulled up to the pier.

What he hadn't expected was the black Ford sedan waiting for him or the lanky Calabrian pacing back and forth, enormous clouds of cigarette smoke wafting in his wake. Valmonte, in the short time Alvorado had known him, had proven to be an impatient man not particularly good at thinking on his feet. He had been tasked with managing his outfit's transfer of operations from Havana to Miami after the Cuba debacle, but what the bosses in New York saw in him Alvorado couldn't guess.

He tossed his cigarette when he spotted Alvorado paying his taxi.

"There you are!" he shouted. "You lousy son of a bitch, I should have Carlo bust your knee! You've got some nerve!"

Alvorado sighed. Every time, without exception.

"What is it this time, Mr. Valmonte?" Alvorado said, walking past him toward the gangplank. "I would have thought you would be pleased that our business is nearly concluded."

"You promised- hey!" Valmonte came running after him, angrily wagging his finger as the man tended to do. His finger was long and bony, like nearly everything else about him. "You promised three animals!"

"Yes, I do believe that was the arrangement," Alvorado said.

"So, you're short-changing me or what?" Valmonte shouted. "I just got done talking with one of your sailors and he tells me there's only two aboard!"

"Mr. Valmonte, I don't know what you're talking about," Alvorado said. "Maybe one of them died en route. It happens. I promised you three animals, I did not promise them alive-"

Valmonte grabbed his arm. The man had a surprisingly strong grip.

"If you-"

"He said nuthin' about no dead lizard," Valmonte hissed. "I swear to God, if you're trying to fuck me..."

Alvorado glared right back. After a long moment he the pried the Calabrian's hand off and boarded the ship. He ignored the man's curses that flew after him.

Captain Pieterman was in his cabin, deep into a bottle of gin and on the last cigarette in the carton he'd picked up in Maracaibo. He'd been leaning in his seat, looking out the window overlooking the pier, watching his sailors go about their jobs.

"Mr. Valmonte is a very pleasant man," Pieterman said dryly as Alvorado stepped inside. "So warm, so inviting..."

"What's this about there being only two animals?" Alvorado said.

Pieterman finished his shot and messily poured himself another.

"You remember your contract," Alvorado said, turning away. "Full payment upon delivery of the Allosauruses, with pay docked thirty-three percent for each animal that doesn't-"

"It's out."

Alvorado froze.

"... What?" he whispered. Pieterman took another swig of gin and sucked a drag from his cigarette.

"Maybe an hour ago," he said, almost monotone. "We were just pulling up to the pier. I don't know, one of my men got careless or made a mistake or...I suppose it doesn't really matter what now. The big one, the one you were calling Jefe, he took the man's arm off. Just a single bite and it was gone. It got on deck - we tried to catch it with the nets - but we were close enough at that point that it just jumped overboard. We watched it make it to shore, I don't think anyone else saw it, but it definitely made it. It was gone by the time we made it here."

Pieterman took another gulp of gin. Alvorado took off his hat and collapsed into the dilapidated sofa beside the cabin door. He could use a drink himself.

"When did he last eat?" Alvorado finally said.

"This afternoon," Pieterman replied. "But you know how these bastards are, that doesn't really matter. Someone will die. Hell, I bet someone already has."

Alvorado let out a long sigh and, reluctantly, nodded.

"How soon can you unload the cargo?" he said.

"Already started," Pieterman said, pouring himself some more gin and gestured toward the window. Alvorado could hear the whirring of a crane. "My men can be done within the hour. Ninety minutes, tops."

"Good." Alvorado stood and opened the door. "Don't wait, get out as soon as you're finished. Go to Nassau, I'll call tomorrow with what to do next."

Assuming he had any idea of what to do by then. Or, hell, if he even made it that long. Alvorado's heart pounded hard in his chest and it wasn't the Floridian humidity making him sweat.

"Of course," Pieterman said, his eyes back on the deck and pier. His sailors were scrambling to get ropes around the crate that concealed an Allosaurus' cage. "What about the Americans?"

"I'll deal with Valmonte," Alvorado said.

"And Jefe?"

Alvorado didn't answer, he just left.

Valmonte was easy enough to satisfy: some story about a clerical mix-up and how the third animal was coming as part of another client's shipment was enough to get the Calabrian to stop asking questions. At least, for now.

Jefe was another matter entirely.

It was well after 11 P.M. when Alvorado got back to the hotel, ignoring the front desk man trying to get his attention and instead going straight up to his room.

Baez picked up on the fourth ring.

"Yeah?"

"We have a problem."

The line crackled silently.

"A Punta Cana problem or a Panama problem?" Baez replied.

"Panama."

Baez spewed a couple rough curses.

"I can be in Miami in twelve hours," Baez said. "How long ago?"

"Two, maybe three hours," Alvorado said. "Called you as soon as I got to a phone."

"Maybe we'll get lucky and it'll just sleep," Baez said. Alvorado sighed, not wanting to even think about the alternative. They agreed to meet at the hotel as soon

as Baez made it to town and ended the call.

What a mess.

This was worse than Panama. At least there they could bribe the locals to keep the whole incident quiet and were lucky enough that the Pterodactyl never wandered into the American zone and only killed a couple of farmers. But, Miami? And a bull Allosaurus at that?

Alvorado raided the suite's mini fridge for liquor and downed a triple shot of Patron. He didn't remember much past that.

He awoke to daylight and Elvis Presley crooning the chorus of "Blue Moon" on the radio in the living room. The radio he might've ignored, but the scent of a freshly lit cigarette shot him straight to full clarity. He quickly snatched his Webley .38 from the nightstand drawer and gingerly slid to the unlatched bedroom door. He peeked through, but all he could see was the shadow of someone sitting in one of the armchairs and the rustle of a magazine page being turned.

Alvorado took a breath, then flung open the door - gun at the ready.

The woman in the armchair smiled and squinted her eyes, perplexed and amused.

"Who did you think was out here?" She spoke with a thick Transatlantic accent, like a Hollywood actress. "Bat Masterson?"

Alvorado let the pistol hang down and flicked the safety back on. She was a tall brunette, light-skinned and amber-eyed. Her sundress was periwinkle and her floppy wide-brimmed hat was white. She crossed her legs and took a soft drag from her cigarette.

"Did Valmonte send you to babysit me?" Alvorado said. She laughed.

"That pencil neck? Good lord, no." She blew a gentle stream of smoke from her nose, the cloud backlit from the window. Looked to be another beautiful day out there, few clouds and loads of sunshine. Just what all the vacationers dreamed of.

"You didn't get our message last night, did you?" she said.

"I'm afraid not." Alvorado pocketed his pistol and walked over to the kitchenette, feeling the first pulses of what was sure to be a hangover. If he was going to be conducting business before breakfast, he could at least use some coffee. "So? Who sent you?"

"Jack."

"I don't know any Jacks."

"Sure you do, honey," she said. She tapped some ash into the tray beside the radio. Alvorado noticed she was reading a copy of Life, the new American president's million-dollar smile plastered all over the cover. "Everybody knows Jack."

Something in Alvorado's brain clicked. He reeled as it brought a new wave of hangover headache along with it.

"...You work for the Old Man," he said.

"Bingo," the woman replied, snuffing out her cigarette. "I like mine black, by the way."

"I don't..."

"You really should've read the telegram, then you wouldn't be so flat-footed." The woman smirked, leaning back in her chair. "Then again..."

"What happened to Arnold?" Alvorado said. "I thought he was the Old Man's point man here?"

"Arnold works for me."

Alvorado sighed and ran a hand through his hair. He could use a shower.

"And you are?"

"Carol," she replied. "Carol Lasseter. But Carol will do. Valmonte runs Mr. Genovese's affairs here, and I manage for Mr. Kennedy."

"If this is about our arrangement..."

"Oh no, the Old Man is quite satisfied," Carol said. "I'm told Bessie really loves Cape Cod. Adapted to the climate even better than hoped."

The electric percolator began to bubble, and the first hints of the rubbish Americans considered coffee began to tickle Alvorado's nostrils.

"No, as I said - Jack sent me," Carol said. "The old man spoke highly of you and your organization and is wondering if you'd be open for another job doing what you do, but this time moving men and materiel. Or, at least he was interested." She rolled her eyes. "Honestly, I doubt it now."

She reached down and fished a newspaper from the white purse on the floor under her feet. Alvorado took it, but felt his gut run cold before he even read the headline:

TERROR IN EDGEWATER

"It sounds like you've got yourself a problem, Luis."

Alvorado pulled a chair and sat at the table.

"I'm taking care of it," he said.

"Now, that I'd like to see," Carol walked to the kitchenette and poured herself a cup. When she saw Alvorado staring she just shrugged. "Don't mind me, do whatever it is you need to do. I can wait."

"So, you're going to babysit me after all."

Carol smiled and sipped her coffee.

"Think of it as an audition."

Two coffees and one icy shower later, Alvorado got the call from Baez. He had no trouble spotting him in the lobby as he got off the elevator, Baez was a hard man to miss: a head taller than everyone else in the room, a thick black horseshoe mustache, dressed in a cream-colored suit and hat. He crossed the room in the time it took Alvorado to take three steps. His expression was grim.

"This is really bad," he hissed. "Worse than Panama."

"I know."

"Panama?" Carol stepped off the elevator, a thin eyebrow raised. "So, this isn't the first time?"

Baez glared. Carol smiled.

"A client," Alvorado said.

Baez was about to put his foot in his mouth when Alvorado shook his head. He kept his mouth shut.

"Well, boys, I hope you have some brilliant plan," Carol said. "Because this isn't Panama and by the looks of it -" She gestured to the other men and women going about their business around them, nearly every single one either carrying or reading a newspaper featuring that "TERROR IN EDGEWATER" headline "-Your pet is now famous."

Alvorado plucked a cigarette from his jacket pocket.

"Alright, let's think a moment," he said, lighting and taking a drag, letting the familiar taste of burning tobacco and menthol soothe his nerves, even if just for a moment. "Based on what the newspaper said, it sounds like the cops don't know yet where Jefe came from. Just speculation that he'd escaped from somewhere."

He started for the exit, the other two following.

"Which means they don't know about the Wanderer," he continued. "So even if they know about us, they can't connect Jefe to us."

"Where are the other two?" Baez said. By the soft gasp she made, Alvorado figured Carol hadn't known that part.

"Valmonte took them," he replied.

"So, he..."

"Unless someone else has another one down here we

don't know about, Valmonte has the only ones," Alvorado said. "Once the cops find that out, he'll be the prime suspect."

"So, you're just going to pin this all on him?" Carol said. "I don't think the Italians are going to like that."

"Someone is going to have to go down for this," Alvorado said. "And I don't plan to be the fall guy. We have to destroy all evidence connecting us to the animal."

He pushed open the door and stepped out into the street. A pair of police cars, sirens screaming, sped past the hotel headed south.

"We'll need the log from the pier," Baez said. "Without that Valmonte can't prove our ship was ever here."

"I can get an alibi," Alvorado said. "That's no problem. But we need that log and we need to point the police in Valmonte's direction. Carol, can you...?"

"I can make a call," she said.

Alvorado sighed a big cloud of smoke. For the first time since Jefe escaped, he felt like he had a handle on the situation.

That's when the gun was shoved into his spine.

Alvorado sighed.

"So that's how it is?" he said.

"What-" Baez started to say before Carol turned the .32 Browning on him. He froze, eyeing the gun and then her.

"Like I said," Carol cooed. "You've got yourself a problem, Luis."

A yellow and white '57 Pontiac Bonneville pulled out of a space a couple of doors down and parked in front of them, the doors swinging open to reveal a pair of swarthy brutes in Cuban hats. The man at the wheel grinned.

"Need a lift?"

"Go on, boys," Carol said. "I won't be far behind."

She pushed the gun into Alvorado's back again. He didn't need to be told twice. He and Baez piled into the back of the car where the second man, just as swarthy as the driver and wearing a poor excuse for a tie with his cheap white polo, kept another gun trained on them. Carol slammed the door shut behind Baez and the car sped off.

The Pontiac turned left and headed west toward the Venetian Causeway. The driver cracked open a window - Alvorado silently thanked God, this thing stunk of sweat and cheap cologne.

"You two work for the Old Man too?" he said. "Or was everything she said bullshit?"

Another police car, siren blaring and lights flashing, swerved around the Pontiac and sped past. It was also headed west.

Both men guffawed. Their laughs reminded Alvorado of wheezing sickly bulldogs. He supposed that was answer enough. The goon to his left poked the barrel of a Colt into Alvorado's ribs. Baez eyed both men.

The Webley .38 was heavy in its holster, under his jacket.

The Pontiac made another turn and they pulled onto the causeway. He could see traffic snarling ahead. Another squealing patrol car rushed past, still in the same direction they were driving.

"You're not taking us to Valmonte," Alvorado said.

"Mr. Valmonte is a busy man," the driver replied.

"He doesn't want to talk?" Alvorado's cigarette was nearly just a nub. "We can talk. It's better for everyone if we just talk."

"Oh, we'll talk," the driver said. The Pontiac slowed to a crawl as it caught up with traffic. "We know a nice place out in the Everglades. Real quiet. We can have ourselves a nice long chat."

Alvorado sat back. The Webley was under his right shoulder. He shared a glance with Baez. Baez tightened his lips and looked at their companion on the opposite side. The gunman grimaced.

"He wants a refund, doesn't he?" Alvorado said. "That's understandable. We can work something out. That's no problem."

It was about timing. The right moment. Just keep talking.

"Why don't we-"

Fire erupted in front of them. The windshield shattered. The driver was screaming.

There were screams everywhere, people scrambling out of their cars and sprinting back east on the causeway. Baez recovered before Alvorado did: he reached into Alvorado's jacket and drew the Webley. BAM! The grunt in the backseat merely watched as Baez put a bullet in his cornea. Muscle memory pulled the trigger on the Colt - it barely missed Alvorado's gut and put a hole in the passenger seat. Baez grabbed Alvorado by the collar and pulled him out of the car.

More gunshots. Alvorado and Baez ducked, turning in

their direction. It was chaos.

Jefe leapt off an overturned and burning patrol car onto a cop.

The man got off one more shot from his service pistol, a pitiful pinprick in the Allosaurus' tough hide, before he was torn in half. Two more cops ducked behind another patrol car and shot at Jefe again, for all the good that would do.

It got his attention.

A mature bull Allosaurus truly was something to see. It was all muscles and teeth, leathery hide and brilliant tiger stripes. Their eyes were cold, like a shark's eyes. Inscrutable. Perhaps there was an intelligence there, but it was alien and indiscernible. Jefe spit out the mauled policeman's torso and howled.

He was not hungry.

He was not angry.

He was having fun.

Jefe opened his jaws in a twisted mock smile. Alvorado and Baez turned and ran.

Alvorado did his best to ignore the blood-dripping shrieks and the staccato of futile gunshots behind him, weaving through the rows of abandoned cars back in the direction of Miami Beach. A bullet slammed into a windshield as he ran by - it was Valmonte's man. His clothes were burnt, and his face was bloody with shrapnel, but he was still kicking unlike his now one-eyed pal.

"Behind us!" Alvorado shouted. Baez didn't miss a beat, spinning and shooting back. His shot flew wide. Valmonte's man didn't stop, still running. His next shot was closer, taking out a passenger window in a Chevy. Alvorado ducked behind a teal Ford convertible.

Another shot. Baez grunted and tripped, his left arm spurting crimson. The Webley vanished somewhere under the Ford.

Valmonte's man weaved around the Chevy, pistol aimed at Baez with Army-trained precision. Baez fumbled, wildly reaching in the wrong direction for the revolver.

Alvorado scrambled on all fours.

There was the Webley! Right next to the front passenger side wheel. He leapt for it, snatching and rolling as the goon circled around the Ford.

Valmonte's man had him.

Too bad Jefe was faster.

The driver managed to get off a couple shots into the Allosaurus' nose before its jaws clamped down on his head, tearing it off as easily as a child might nibble off the tip of a banana. Blood and gore gushed in the moments it took the man's body to realize it was dead.

Alvorado was on his feet, even though he didn't remember standing. Jefe looked at him with unblinking eyes, dripping sinew hanging from his teeth. Alvorado dropped the revolver and backed away slowly, hesitantly. He looked right into Jefe's eyes, but they were as clear as obsidian. The Allosaurus tilted his head, but that was all.

"Luis..."

Baez had propped himself against the Ford and wrapped his wound with his tie. Alvorado pulled him to his feet, never breaking eye contact with Jefe.

The Allosaurus snorted and blinked.

He'd never seen one blink before.

A particularly brave pelican squawked a challenge, which Jefe thought was more worth his attention. He turned away. Alvorado and Baez fled.

The cops had already blocked off the bridge by the time they reached shore, their lungs burning and Baez deathly pale as he collapsed into the arms of an officer. It took a second to stop them from toppling over.

"Anyone else?"

Alvorado barely registered the question. His chest and cheeks were prickly and numb.

"Mister!" All Alvorado noticed of the cop was his wrinkled forehead and blonde stubble. "Is there anyone else on the bridge?"

Alvorado shook his head. He weakly pointed at Baez.

"Ricochet..." he gasped, "Ricochet..."

"Howie! Come over here, let's get this guy out of here."

It was as they helped him to his feet again that Alvorado realized how many people surrounded him: a small army of cops armed with shotguns and Thompson submachine guns, a growing crowd of gaping onlookers, ambulances and people tending to the wounded. He watched them help Baez to a gurney.

"Son, you alright?"

Alvorado nodded. He reached for his hat, only now noticing he'd lost it somewhere in the jumble.

"I'm fine, just fine, thanks," he said. In the distance Jefe howled. "Just, just shaken is all."

"Glad to hear it," the cop said, offering a smile and a slap on the shoulder. "Better get back, then."

The cop turned away and forgot Alvorado existed.

He'd walked at least a block, maybe more, when he collapsed onto the stoop of some bodega and, hands shaking violently, fished a half-crushed cigarette from his pocket. Thank Christ he hadn't lost his lighter too.

Halfway through his second smoke, the shaking stopped. He was well into his third when he started to think of what to do next.

Turning the cops onto Valmonte was still his best play. That, at least, he was pretty sure of how to pull off. The problem was figuring out how to prevent Valmonte from turning around and pointing the finger back his way. He had to assume everything he said to Carol she'd told Valmonte, which probably meant the Italians had the logbook by now.

Alvorado tossed the spent cigarette and hailed a cab. One thing at a time.

"South beach," Alvorado said. "Eleventh and Ocean."

"Seriously?" The driver had a terrible combover. "Buddy, haven't you heard? Not a great day for the beach."

Alvorado passed him a couple bills. The man shrugged and did as he was told.

The Whitecrest Hotel had seen better days. It had always been mob owned, but as New York's interest shifted down to Havana it had become ignored and left to fall apart. Since the communists took over they'd hastily shifted their assets back here and placed Valmonte, the brother-in-law of somebody worthwhile up in Brooklyn, in charge while they got their bearings. He'd kept the lights on, but wasn't exactly a shred businessman.

Alvorado couldn't be sure where Valmonte had brought the other two Allosauruses. The Italians had a collection of properties throughout South Florida that could easily hide them. But, he figured, considering Valmonte probably hadn't found out about Jefe's rampage until it made the papers, he had probably not thought it necessary to hide the animals at all until this morning. Which likely meant he had simply had them trucked from the Wanderer straight to the indoor

enclosure he'd built in the Whitecrest's new addition, where the animals were supposed to take up residence as the hotel's latest attraction - a nice stopgap until his bosses bribed enough state officials to get gambling legalized here.

Valmonte needed them gone, but it was probably too risky to move them before sundown. The Whitecrest made the most sense.

Alvorado circled around the back and did his best to blend into the pedestrian traffic, walking up Ocean Court and keeping an eye out for a back entrance big enough. Sure enough: the new addition had its own loading dock and parked right in front of it were two box trucks - the same on ones he recalled pulling up to the pier as he left the Wanderer the night before.

He walked south one more block, then stopped in a luncheonette and walked straight to the phone booth in the back.

Arnold Forsythe picked up on the fourth ring.

"Luis?" he said. He sounded very surprised to hear from him. "Jesus, I heard on the radio..."

"Yeah, I know," Alvorado said. "I need a favor."

"Is Carol with you? We haven't heard from her all day."

"...She really does work for the Old Man?"

"Of course," Arnold said, "For the last five years. What the hell's going on?"

Alvorado heard the luncheonette's front door tingle. The cook tossed another burger on the grill and the place filled with the aroma of burning beef.

"Listen," he said. "The Whitecrest. I need you to-"

Ah, the familiar prodding of a gun barrel against his spine. Alvorado immediately hung up.

"Who was that?"

Alvorado didn't recognize the voice but recognized the accent and the shadow.

"Nobody, Carlo."

"Cops?"

"I'm not stupid, No."

Carlo grunted.

"What did you tell 'em?"

"Only where you'll be taking me," Alvorado replied. "Didn't have a chance to say more."

Valmonte was waiting in the Whitecrest's loading dock, pacing and puffing away impatiently like he was the night before. Daylight did his looks no favors, just accentuating the appearance of a needle-nosed twig. At least his white dinner jacket looked merely like a Clark Gable hand-me-down rather than something fished out of the bargain bin at the corner thrift shop.

Two burly men in chocolate suspenders and ties shooed away a pair of unsuspecting nobodies.

"You've got some DAMN nerve!" The Calabrian wagged his finger like a big band conductor. "Where the hell are Nico and Ernie?"

Alvorado shrugged innocently.

"Who?"

That earned him a jab in the kidneys. Valmonte grabbed him by the shirt. The man's breath stunk of tobacco and sambuca.

"You lie to me? You try to fuck me? Me?" he hissed. "You're nothing, a god damned roach!"

Valmonte shoved him away. He spat out his cigarette and was quick to light another.

"I want a refund," he growled. "I'm getting a damn refund and getting rid of these fucking lizards. I ain't going to prison because of your fuck up."

He blew a cloud of smoke in Alvorado's face.

"But not from you."

Alvorado smirked.

"Good luck with that, amigo."

Valmonte turned away.

"Carlo," he said. "How about you re-acquaint this fella with his wares?"

Carlo chuckled and shoved Alvorado toward a small side door.

"Sure, boss," he said. "I bet the ladies could use an afternoon snack."

Alvorado's stomach churned. Even if Arnold had understood his message, there was no way he'd get here in time.

The Whitecrest's Allosaurus enclosure reminded

Alvorado of an operating theater: a gallery of stadium style seats and benches overlooking a dugout space, dolled up with jungle foliage and rocks, lit from above by a glass skylight and electric spotlights.

A mix of stale skin and foul rot slapped him in the face as he entered the room. He knew that stench well.

One of the cow Allosauruses looked up as Carlo shoved him to the rim. The two lizards were stretched out lazily in the center of the pit, like bored tomcats in the afternoon sun.

"come on, come on," Carlo chuckled. "Over that way." He shoved Alvorado again, this time toward a break in the retaining wall circling the pit. The goon fished out a key, tiny brass in Carlo's sausage fingers, and unlatched a padlocked gate blocking off a ladder that descended into the enclosure. He kicked the gate open and pointed his pistol at Alvorado's gut.

"Go on," he said. "Don't keep 'em waiting."

"Carlo, listen..."

Carlo cocked his pistol.

"I ain't askin' twice, Ritchie Valens," he growled.

Alvorado glanced down into the pit again: both Allosauruses were watching now, their jaws hanging open just enough to reveal the steak knives that lined their gums. He eyed Carlo's pistol. Could he take him before he fired a shot? The barrel swayed casually and deliberately toward the gate. Alvorado loosened his tie. He cursed silently and stepped onto the first rung.

"You ever seen one of these things eat?" Alvorado said.

"No," Carlo replied. "But I've seen a man get mauled

by a gator before. I imagine it ain't much different."

Alvorado stepped down to the second rung.

"You'd think so," Alvorado said. He guessed Carlo was standing two, no, three feet away. "They're faster, messier. These things tear through men like they were made of whipped cream. But, not immediately. They think about it, toy with the idea for a bit. More like a frog contemplating a fly."

"Huh," Carlo said as Alvorado stepped down once more. He lowered his pistol a bit, his aim now just off. "Sounds like-"

Now!

Alvorado snatched at Carlo's ankle and hopped off the ladder. The man yelped! Bits of shattered cement sprayed into Alvorado's face as a bullet slammed into the retaining wall, the ricochet grazing his neck. Carlo fell hard, slid, and flailed - his hands found nothing to hold. Both men fell.

Something cracked loudly as they landed, and the pain nearly turned Alvorado blind. He rolled, scrambling dizzily for his feet. They had landed a yard from the ladder... Everything moved. His head felt like mush.

The Allosauruses stood.

Alvorado threw himself at the ladder. He made up only two rungs before Carlo grabbed him by the collar and tore him off. He guessed he'd been punched when he came to a moment later on his back seeing double. Carlo, blood drizzling from his ear and busted brow, hadn't made it much further up than he had - Alvorado grabbed his leg again and pulled. Carlo just kicked him in the nose with his other foot.

The Allosauruses watched the scene, curious, closer and closer, their footsteps ginger and soft.

Alvorado ignored the copper taste in his mouth and looked for something, anything. He hurled a softball-sized rock at Carlo's head - he missed, but managed to nick his right hand instead. Carlo cursed as he lost his grip and fell again. Alvorado was atop him in a flash, swinging his fists in short desperate jabs to Carlo's temples. When Valmonte's goon tried to throw him off, Alvorado smashed him in the jaw with his elbow.

Both men were suddenly in shadow.

Alvorado flew up the ladder in a panic, Carlo's bloody screams chasing after him. He heaved himself over the top and out of the pit in time to hear limbs torn and the crunch of a human skull in an Allosaurus' jaws. He lay on the floor, aching and gasping raggedly.

Something was burning.

"Very impressive, Luis, very impressive."

Carol Lasseter stood over him, watching the folded paper sheets she held between her fingers slowly smolder. She tossed them over the side of the retaining wall and they vanished, ashes scattering over the pit.

If he had the strength to strangle her, he would. She must've seen the fury in his eyes: she pursed her lips in a mock pout.

"Oh, don't be like that," she said. "It had to play out that way. I knew the Italians were watching, and if there was any hope for you I couldn't be picked up too. Besides, you got away, didn't you? Your friend took a little lead, but nothing he won't walk away from."

She sat in one of the theater seats, crossed her legs, and smiled.

Alvorado groaned. He forced himself to sit up, leaning back to rest against the retaining wall.

"Great, so you screwed me for my own benefit," he said. "I suppose you expect me to thank you for nearly getting eaten and shot twice today."

She picked out a cigarette from her purse and offered it. He let her poke it between his lips and light - the menthol was just the sort of soothing he needed about now.

"Now what?" he said.

"Now the boys in blue cart Valmonte away, just as you said." She lit a cigarette for herself. "I expect they'll pick him up at the airport, I doubt he realizes the arrest warrant's already been issued. An uppity gangster gone rogue, got sloppy, and that'll be all the papers will care to write."

"Convenient," Alvorado said. He breathed out the wisps of burnt menthol and tobacco slowly. His right leg had gone completely numb. He figured either a broken hip or thigh.

"Very much so," Carol replied. "A shame we'll never quite figure out how he got the animals into Miami. The cops will be scratching their fat heads for years. Thank goodness we had an undercover G-Man already in place to blow the whistle on the whole thing."

Alvorado mulled that one over. Carol looked up as the doors opened and the sounds of men storming in echoed throughout the theater.

"Holy cow!"

"Get a load of that! Two more of 'em!"

From the pit, one of the Allosauruses hissed loudly.

"Hello boys, over here," Carol called, waving a hand, "There's an injured man, I think he's a government man. Better call a doctor."

Carol leaned down, smiling again.

"We can catch up later," she whispered.

Alvorado sighed, listening as those boots stomped closer. It was about time he retired from dinosaur smuggling anyway. Surely playing spy games would pay better.

Maricomboese Sausage

It's a matter of well-known record that the people of the Maricombo Valley have practices and beliefs which stretch the definition of "natural" to a point well beyond any useful meaning. The Maricomboese practice of the dark arts was something Professor Alton had spent much of his life devoted to studying, and it was no secret on campus that the man had become a tad deranged over the years because of it. He was rarely seen outside the classroom, and was rumored to live out of a small room attached to his office by a corridor hidden from view to visitors by a large set of metal shelves covered in the still undocumented and forgotten prizes of his last venture to the Congo.

They found his body, sans head and limbs, under the

highway overpass crossing the Miskatonic River.

The police came to question David that afternoon. As the graduate assistant assigned to his class the night before, he quickly reached the top of the list among those who'd last seen Alton alive.

"So, did you see anything out of the ordinary?" the detective, clearly a Boston transplant of some sort, said. "Really, anything you have to say or remember will be useful."

"Do you mean, 'more out of the ordinary than usual?'" David replied. The detective sighed, reaching for the quickly cooling cup of Krispy Kreme coffee.

"Yeah, that," he said. "I've gotten a good idea of how odd Alton was."

"Have you?" David said. He leaned back in his leather desk chair. "Because the professor really was into some fucked up shit."

"Yeah, well, I guess you've got to be a little screwy to spend your life studying this Mary...Murray..."

"Maricomboese."

"Yeah, that," The detective said, taking a sip of his latte. "The Dean gave us a brief summary."

"Alton was the expert, the worldwide authority," David said. "You weren't going to find anything or anyone that had more info on the subject than him. But..."

The detective leaned forward.

"Well, to get that information, he was willing to go to places and do things most wouldn't dare. The way he talked about some of this..." David said. "The human sacrifice rituals? The cannibalism? I'd swear he was speaking from experience."

"Well, the Dean said he'd spent years-"

"No, not from observation," David said. "Like, he'd done it. Not just done it, as if he was a practitioner."

The detective grimaced, stroking his chin.

"I never had proof, just...a feeling," David said. "Sometimes, there would be people, I never knew who they were, who would show up after class. I'd say they were friends of his, but it's hard to imagine Alton had any friends, you know?"

The detective took out his notebook.

"Can you describe them?" he said.

"White," David said. "Middle aged. One was an older man, probably close to Alton's age. Just...kinda normal looking people. But, they seemed to know a lot about the Maricomboese stuff. I overheard him chatting with them about it."

David chatted with the detective for another hour or so before he left, leaving his card in case they thought of anything more.

Maybe a week later David got a news alert on his phone: three people, a middle aged couple from Amesbury and their friend, a dentist from Danvers, had been arrested in connection with Alton's murder. A fourth, a 70-year old supermarket manager, was also suspected but had committed suicide shortly after the police had first questioned him. It seemed like an open and shut case as far as the Essex County prosecutor's office was concerned.

David put his iPhone down and returned to his dinner. The sausage was excellent. It really was a shame.

Across the Sea

"Have you ever wondered what's on the other side?"

Chetla looked up from stoking the campfire and shot a quizzical glance toward Ichabalac. The night was young and humid, the stars visible but the sky not quite dark yet. The air was thick with sea salt and brine, the crash of ocean waves on the beach a steady constant.

"Not really," Chetla said and shrugged. "Other islands, I guess. It's just the sea, after all."

"Well, yeah, I know that," Ichabalac said, laying back on the sand.

Satisfied that the fire was a healthy one, Chetla snatched one of the w wineskins they'd brought with them and plopped onto the sand beside Ichabalac. He took a swig of wine, then offered it - Ichabalac took a big gulp himself. They were well on their way to hangovers come dawn.

"How many times have you been to Buko?" Ichabalac said.

"I think this is maybe my third or fourth," Chetla said, his eyes fixed on a seagull bobbing on a wave several yards offshore. "Father says because I'm almost a man that I need to become familiar with the King's Court."

Ichabalac handed the wineskin back. Chetla took another gulp - it was sweet, but dry and burned the throat. And, hoo-boy, it helped make the world's problems just fade away.

"I suppose that makes sense," Ichabalac said. "My father says the same. That I need to tag along so I can be a better bodyguard for you."

"You mean my brother," Chetla said, rolling his eyes. "I'll probably just end up another spearman like you."

"I hope not!" Ichabalac laughed. "You'd be a pretty terrible warrior."

Chetla sighed, took another swing, then passed back the wineskin.

"You know, I wouldn't mind finding out what's on the other side of the sea," Chetla said. "If we built a big enough boat, who knows how far we could go?"

"Well, there's the stories about the sea people..."

"Oh, the humans?"

"Yeah," Ichabalac said. "What's the place they come from? Aotearoa? It's supposed to be gigantic. Like, you could walk for days and days and days and never see -" HIC! "-the sea at all."

Chetla smiled. The last hints of sunset were almost gone from the sky, leaving nothing but the quarter moon and Milky Way.

"I'd love to see that."

= = =

Chetla awoke with the overwhelming aroma of burning wood clogging his nostrils and a distant voice calling his name. After a minute or so laying in that haze between the sleeping and waking world, he realized the voice wasn't his imagination - someone back down the beach really was calling out for him and Ichabalac. He sat up, but did so too quickly and was overwhelmed by the pounding headache he'd been too tired to notice.

"Ugh..." he grumbled, clutching his temples. "How much did we drink...?"

Ichabalac was still snoring away, his face buried under his arms as hey lay on his stomach. Chetla nudge him with his knee. Ichabalac's tail gave an annoyed twitch and he groaned.

"Hey, get up," Chetla said, squinting at the figure sprinting their way. "I think you father's come for us."

That got him up.

Ichabalac shot to his feet and by the time Ohozachulito reached them he was standing at attention, his eyes bloodshot and clearly suffering from as bad a hangover but doing his best not to make it obvious.

Ohozachulito was too out of breath to really pay much attention to those details. He wasn't an old man, but he'd been the captain of Anize's spearmen for Chetla's father for longer than he could remember and certainly looked the part of a grizzled old warrior. Save for the lack of scars and broken headfrills, Ichabalac was more or less a more youthful spitting image of him. It was because Ichabalac's father served Chetla's that the two met and became friends at all.

"Sheezu be praised," Ohozachulito gasped. "You're both alright! After last night, I feared the worst…"

"Last night…?" Chetla said, still sitting in the sand cradling his head. Maybe if he just lay back down the pounding would stop…

Ohozachulito bowed to Chetla.

"Forgive me, Young Lord, but much has happened," he said. "Buko has been attacked. The King is dead."

= = =

The fires were out but the heavy still thick with the smell of burnt wood and palm as Chetla, Ichabalac, and Ohozachulito re-entered Buko.

Buko, being well within Zuazubo territory, wasn't a walled town. It straddled the southern coast of the harbor, a haphazard collection of huts, farms, and markets centered around two points: the docks along the coast and the Temple of Sheezu a mile or two inland. Buko, well before the Palm Clan came to rule the kingdom, was just a fishing community and at heart it still was even though in the decades since it became the royal court it has more than doubled in size.

"What happened here?" Chetla said.

Ohozachulito sighed. He was still a fit and able fighter, but for the first time Chetla really noticed how old he'd become. Since when were the wrinkles around his eyes so pronounced?

"They came overnight," he said. "Fifty, I think. Maybe a hundred. They came by sea, must have, there was no other way for them to have gotten so many so close. Probably came ashore a few miles south and then waited for dark before attacking."

As the three walked deeper into the town, there was less evidence of an attack but more people distraught and in mourning. Everyone had painted the traditional black stripe over their eyes - Chetla and Ichabalac had used ashes from their campfire until they could actually touch up their body paint.

"When the attack began," Ohozachulito said. "The King and his sons were among the first to ush to Buko's defense. But, Choum be damned, they were also among the first to fall. We fought as best we could, but our will was broken. By the time we rallied, the battle was already lost and our enemy had vanished again into the night."

"A raid?" Ichabalac said. "Who were they? Pirates?"

"No way," Chetla said. "There are no pirates so bold!"

They at last reached the Temple of Sheezu - six stone columns, arranged in a square, surrounding the only all-stone building in Buko: the blue and white Shrine to the Goddess Sheezu. A crowd of people were gathered outside: some praying, some in mourning, and some who looked to just be waiting. But for what?

Ohozachulito stopped.

"I can think of one…" Ohozachulito said. "Zohd."

Chetla glanced toward Ichabalac, but he was just as clueless.

"Who?" Chetla said.

"His real name is Ehezodho," Ohozachulito said. "Once upon a time, he was expected to be King of Ooyovu. But, he was a cruel and terrible prince who would torture and kill just for his own amusement. Have you heard of the war between Ichaba and Ooyovu? You may be too young to remember it, but that was started by one of Zohd's bloody escapades. That war was the last straw - his father and younger siblings disowned him and forced him to flee Ooyovu. Ever since, he's been a scourge: kidnapping fishermen, raiding villages not just on Jujo but all over the islands. But, if this was him, he's never before been so bold…"

Chetla was about to ask more when a voice shouted his name. They turned to find the Lord of Anize - bruised and battered after the battle, but no worse than that.

"Father!" Chetla said, running to embrace him.

"Oh, thank the Goddess," he said, holding Chetla tight. "I feared the worst...I couldn't...not both of you…"

Chetla pulled away.

"Both?"

He looked around, but his father was alone.

"Father," Chetla said. "Where is Chak?"

He opened his mouth to speak, but could manage no more than a croak. He embraced Chetla again.

"My son…"

“Father,” Chetla said again. “Where is my brother?”

His father took a breath, but did not let Chetla go.

“They took him,” he at last whispered. “Your brother is gone.”

= = =

Night had settled on Buko, a tense darkness with the memories of the previous night still fresh in everyone's minds. The day had passed in a blur for Chetla, a whirlwind of faces and emotions in the hours since he learned of Chak's kidnapping. Chak and Chetla had not been the closest of siblings, Chak was years older and as the heir to their father always had the greater responsibility. Still, despite the rivalries and the pettiness of their bickering, he never hated his brother. 'Love' may be too strong a word to describe his feelings, but he certainly never wanted his brother killed or...worse.

Being taken prisoner and enslaved by the most brutal of all pirates certainly qualified as worse.

"No."

Ichabalac looked up, surprised. It was the first thing Chetla had said in hours.

"I don't accept this," Cheta whispered. The two were alone now, Ichabalac having finally pulled Chetla away from the seemingly endless summit of lords and warriors discussing what to do next. They had wandered the streets in silence for a while, before finally ending up in the port. They were sitting on a dock now, letting their feet hang off and the sea foam tickle their toes.

"I don't know if this is really something you need to accept or not," Ichabalac said. "He's gone."

"He's not DEAD!" Chetla said. "Everyone talks as if Zohd has already killed him. Chak is alive, I know he is. I...I won't leave him."

Ichabalac grinned.

"That's the spirit!" he said, pulling himself up and hopping to his feet. "Screw all these old people and their endless talking."

Ichabalac offered his hand. Chetla grinned back, took it, and let himself be pulled back up.

"We're going to do it," Chetla said. "Let's do this!"

"I go where you go," Ichabalac said. "What's the plan?"

Chetla stroked his chin.

"Well, we've got our spears already," He said. "So all we really need is a canoe and some idea of where to go..."

Ichabalac looked past Chetla, spotting something.

"I've got a feeling they might know."

Chetla turned: only a hundred yards away, two people were loading a large canoe with spears, shields, and what looked to be an army's worth of arrows. From this far and in the dark neither Chetla nor Ichabalac could make out faces, but clearly the two were trying to work in secret considering the dark cloaks they had wrapped their heads and bodies in.

"Perhaps we should say hello?" Ichabalac said.

Chetla grinned again.

"Perhaps we should give them a hand?"

The mysterious pair were so engrossed in their work they didn't notice Chetla and Ichabalac until they were practically in the boat with them. One of then immediately grabbed a shark-toothed sword and pointed it threateningly at them.

"Who goes there?"

Chetla stopped less due to the threat and more out of surprise - the voice was far younger and far more feminine than he had expected.

"I am Chetla of Anize. Who are you?"

"Anize?"

The other figure, still in the canoe, looked up at them.

"You are the younger brother, aren't you?" The voice was just as young as Chetla and Ichabalac, but while as feminine sounded somehow less so than her companion. It was a voice used to commanding, not to answering inquiries. "The Lord of Anize's other son."

"I am," Chetla said. "And this is a friend. Who are you?"

The woman in the boat climbed back onto the dock and pulled back her cloak. Chetla's heart skipped a beat while Ichabalac gasped. Both immediately knelt.

"Princess Uvajeopa!"

"I'm tired of these old men standing around and talking nonsense, waiting for either my younger brother or my uncle to get here while my father's and brothers' murderers escapes justice and our people are at his mercy."

"We feel exactly the same, your highness,"Chetla said.

Uvajeopa grinned.

"Then, get in the boat," she said. "We have no time to waste. Ocadopa?"

"Yes, my lady?" Uvajeopa's bodyguard said, the sword

vanishing beneath her cloak.

"Cast off."

= = =

Zohd's hideout was a rock jutting out of the sea, a sharp and barren stone miles from anything. An army would need hundreds of spearmen and archers to take it - at least. As the princess put it, the rock had already survived at least two sieges already by Zohd's enemies, both ending in bloody victory for the pirate. Against the cloudless blue midday sky and the near endless sea surrounding it, Zohd's island looked like a stark escapee of a twisted dream. It was disarmingly serene and unnervingly still. Other than the rhythm of the waves and the seagulls overhead, nothing moved.

It all gave Chetla chills.

"Don't lose your nerves now," Uvajeopa said. She must have a natural sense for weakness.

Chetla gripped his paddle more tightly and tried harder to cover up his fear. Despite their bravado the night before, neither Ichabalac nor Chetla had ever been in battle before. They had trained, sure, and Chetla would be the first to say that Ichabalac had done so harder (and better), but nothing real.

He felt Ichabalac's hand on his shoulder. He looked back to find his friend's reassuring smile. Chetla tried to smile back and nodded. Together.

While an army might not be able to take Zohd's rock, a party as small as theirs would have no trouble sneaking in. They found a tiny cove, away from what they supposed was the pirates' main mooring and dragged their canoe ashore, hiding it behind a small outcropping.

"Right there," Uvajeopa said. "Take what you can and we'll climb up there."

She pointed toward a hard, but not impossible, part of the cliff face.

"We?" Ichabalac said.

"Yes, we," Uvajeopa snapped, her words salted with righteous fury. "I did not come all this way just to watch the waves."

Ichabalac shared a look with Ocadopa.

"Forgive me for speaking out of turn, your highness," the princess' bodyguard said. "But I can understand his concern. We've already lost a king and two princes, the kingdom and the tribe would be even more heartbroken to lose a queen too."

That, word, 'queen', hung in the air a long moment.

The king's death was so recent, the emotions so high after the attack, that the reality of just who Uvajeopa was hadn't occurred to Chetla. There had not been a queen of the Zuazubo in generations, but as the eldest surviving child and one of such fierce spirit...

"I told you before we began this expedition, that is a risk I am willing to take."

"Your highness..." Chetla started, but Uvajeopa cut in:

"My father died leading our warriors from the front. I will not dishonor him by failing to do the same."

Ichabalac and Ocadopa sighed. Chetla nodded.

"If that is all," the princess said, heft a sack of arrows

over her shoulder. "Then let's begin."

Chetla looked up at the cliff, a good thirty feet at least and gulped. Could he really climb that? Without the pirates noticing.

The next thing he remembered, he was already at the top, gasping for breath, in disbelief that he had done it. He looked out over the ocean and only now did it strike him that this was the first time he had ever left his island, and as hard as he squinted he could not see even a shadow of it on the horizon.

They might as well be on another world.

He didn't have long to contemplate: the silence of the island was broken by a sneeze. The four froze a moment, each looking to the other with the same question on their minds. When the sneeze was immediately followed by the telltale click-scratch of toe claws on stone, they all knew the answer. they scrambled to hide wherever they could.

They didn't have long to wait.

Only a couple of minutes passed before the culprit shambled into view: He was no more than ten or fifteen years older than them, the scars that crisscrossed his arms and chest made clear he had seen more than his fair share of battle. He walked with a slight limp, not a handicap but at a guess just store feet. The pirate had a chipped battle axe strapped to his hip, but it was a flask of some drink he held in his hands. Wine, Chetla guessed, based on how eagerly he drank and the belch that followed.

The pirate stopped, no more than twenty yards away.

Chetla held his breath. Had they been found already?

An eternity passed.

The pirate belched again.

"Ugh, stupid," he grumbled. The pirate walked past the boulder Ichabalac and Ocadopa had hidden behind - the two silently slid around to the opposite side as he passed and sat on a smaller rock right at the edge, letting his feet hang over the cliff. He took another long swig of wine.

"So stupid," he grumbled again, lost in his own world.

From the relative safety of his hiding place, Chetla signaled Ichabalac.

"What do we do now?" he mouthed. Ichabalac shrugged. He whispered to Ocadopa. She mimed tip-toeing with her fingers, then made a pushing gesture. Ichabalac looked over at the pirate, took a step forward, but then shook his head and hid again.

To Chetla's left, atop the largest outcropping in sight, Uvajeopa crawled into view. Carefully, quietly, she drew an arrow from her sack and notched it. She waited a long moment - Chetla feared the pirate would turn suddenly and spot her - before finally raising her bow. She pulled the drawstring back and aimed - steady at first, but the longer she hesitated the more shaky her hands became. At last, she lowered her bow again and ducked back down.

Chetla exhaled. He didn't even realize he was holding his breath again.

The pirate suddenly shot to his feet.

"Huh? Who's there?"

Chetla's heart practically stopped then and there. He ducked back behind the boulder, his back pressed to it so tightly he might as well have become one with it. He heard the pirate draw his axe and walk toward him, firmly, decisively.

"I know you're there, come-"

THUNK!

The pirate took a couple of wobbly steps and then fell shoulder-first into the boulder, slid, and finally landed face -down at Chetla's feet. Chetla hopped away, startled. Ichabalac, holding his spear like a club, let his arms rest at his sides and gapped for breath.

"Is...is he...?"

Uvajeopa was beside them in an eyeblink, holding the pirate down while Ocadopa tied his hands behind his back.

"Good work!" she said. "He's out cold."

Ichabalac breathed a sigh of relief.

"It won't be long before he's missed," Ocadopa said. "Which way did he come from?"

"That way I think," Chetla said, pointing south.

"They don't know we're here," Uvajeopa said. "If we're going to save your brother and the others taken, now is the time."

Chetla nodded.

The four sprinted south.

= = =

Zohd's camp was at the center of the island, in the middle of a dry lake bed. While the high cliffs surrounding the camp served as a natural fortification, they were jagged and filled with small crevices that a small party could sneak through. The pirates expected an army, though, not four teenage novices.

Chetla and the others snuck through one of these unguarded passages north of the camp and quietly made their way along the shadows toward a higher point so they could get a better idea of what they were up against.

"I see them!" Ichabalac said, doing his best not to shout. He pointed toward the eastern end of the camp and what, at first, looked like a bunch of fenced in boars. Chetla squinted - his sight from this far wasn't as good as Ichabalac's - and realized that his friend was right: it was the prisoners, each wearing burlap bags over their heads, sitting with hands and feet bound. Around the fences he could see two or three guards posted, though from this far it was hard to tell if any were really paying attention to anything. One looked asleep, another looked to be well on his way to a drunken stupor.

"How do we get to them?" Chetla said. "We might be able to get past those guards, but not before one of the others spot us."

"We'll have to create a distraction," Uvajeopa said.

"I can handle that, your highness," Ocadopa said, bowing. "Leave it to me."

"Better make it quick," Ichabalac said, pointing in the direction they'd just come. "I think they've noticed their friend is missing."

They looked: several of the pirates had gathered on the north end of the camp and were having what looked to be a very lively conversation, occasionally pointing and gesturing toward the north end of the island. Two more ran over, both wielding clubs, and together the group started walking north.

"We won't have much time, then," Uvajeopa said. Ocadopa nodded and, without another word, climbed back down and started toward the camp. The other three, carefully, moved through the shadows again, closer toward the prisoners.

Then, they waited.

"What sort of distraction is she going to make?" Chetla said.

Uvajeopa just smiled.

A moment later, Chetla got a whiff of smoke and a commotion erupted on the opposite side of the camp.

"There's your answer," Ichabalac said. "Come on!"

The three sprinted from their hiding place toward the corral. One of the guards noticed them, but before he could call for help Ichabalac dove, feet first, at him, swiping his spear at the pirate's legs as he slid past. The guard fell, face first, and before he had a chance to regain his senses Chetla followed up with a sing at the back of his head with the blunt end of his own weapon. It made a sickening crack against the pirates head, and then he was still.

No time to wonder about it.

Only a few yards away was a gate, held shut by a thick ropes tied in a knot around the posts. It took three strong slashes of Chetla's spear and a little bit of sawing by Ichabalac's knife to cut through them, but they were cut and the gate was open. The three immediately rushed to the prisoners, pulling sacks off their heads and slicing off their bindings.

"Quiet! Quiet!" Uvajeopa hissed. "And quickly!"

They were nearly through them all when the pirates

realized what was happening.

A horn sounded.

A dozen pirates, heavily scarred Ookochu wielding clubs and hand axes, descended on the corral - without hesitation, Ichabalac raced to meet them, followed close behind by maybe a dozen of the Zuazubo tribesmen and women they'd just freed, rushing to battle even unarmed. Chetla handed his knife to the young woman he'd just freed and raced to join them.

Immediately, Chetla was lost amid the chaos.

He saw Ichabalac duck away as one pirate swung his club at him, and in one swift motion knock the same pirate senseless with the butt of his spear.

He saw one of prisoners leap at another pirate, attempting to wrestle his captor to the ground, only for yet another brute to slam his axe into the center of the poor man's back. He fell, bloody.

He saw another couple of the prisoners pick up rocks and throw them at the pirates, one stone smashed into a pirate's forehead and he collapsed, clutching at his face.

He saw a yellow-eyed pirate raise his club and -

Oh! He was coming at HIM!

Chetla was beside himself, or at least it felt as if he were, watching as he dodged the attack and slashed at the pirate with his spear, slicing a deep gash across the Ookochu's chest and arm. The pirate grunted, clutching at his wounds, and backed away - Chetla pressed the advantage, hopping forward and throwing a punch. His right fist collided with the pirate's jaw with a loud crunch, and a bolt of pain shot from Chetla's wrist up his forearm.

Chetla yelped, but the pirate fell, out cold.

Chetla turned, the adrenaline from the encounter still rushing, only to find another pirate already descending on him, an axe over his head, falling -

THUNK!

An arrow suddenly buried itself deep into the pirate's chest. Eyes wide with shock, the pirate dropped his axe, twisted to the side, and fell at Chetla's feet.

Nearby, Uvajeopa was already notching another arrow and taking aim at another opponent.

"ENOUGH!"

The voice broke through the din of the battle and stopped everyone in their tracks. They turned toward the owner and the crowd parted, revealing an ookochu who towered over all others - in presence, at least, if not literally. He was handsome with the sort of face that would make ladies swoon and other men jealous, his eyes had a fire Chetla had never seen before. He walked like a man who had never had to step aside for another, and like a man who had slit the throat of the last who had tried to make him do so.

It was Zohd.

Zohd, all eyes at last on him, grinned - a vicious sneer of a smile - and heaved a blood-smeared club over his right shoulder. He wore shoulder guards carved from bone, and twin bandoliers of throwing knives crisscrossed his chest. Behind him, a tail missing its last few inches swished with satisfied, confident movements. At his feet, a young ookochu lay, his head beaten from where Zohd's club had struck, one of his head fins broken and half hanging from the back of his head.

A chill ran down Chetla's spine. It was Ichabalac.

"Very nice, hatchlings, very nice," Zohd said. "But I'm afraid your little game is quite over."

Uvajeopa notched an arrow and aimed toward the pirate prince.

"Now, now, little lady," Zod said, stepping on Ichabalac's back. He groaned, but did not resist. "Put the bow down or your little friend may find himself short one head."

"I'll put the bow down once you let all the rest go," she said. "Or once my arrow is lodged in your eye. Either, or."

Zohd smacked his lips and feigned heartbreak.

"Oh, my dear, such harsh words!" he said, placing a hand over his heart in mock surprise. "What did I ever do to deserve such as this?" He sneered again, the lines in his face and snout growing very clear and menacing. "Did I kill someone you love?"

Uvajeopa grimaced.

"Oh, I did, didn't I?" he cheerfully hissed. "Who was it? A lover? No...a brother? Two, maybe? Or maybe it was your father?"

His eyes lit up and he let loose a terrible laugh, an unnerving high-pitch squeal. It reminded Chetla of a distressed boar.

"Princess Uvajeopa, I presume?" he said at last.

The princess said nothing. Instinct drove Chetla to raise his spear and move to her side.

"How precious," Zohd said. He snapped his fingers. "Bring her to me."

The pirates, all of them, charged.

= = =

In those moments after the pirates began their charge, a storm of thoughts coursed through Chetla's mind. He thought of his mother, whose last words to him before leaving Anize were to keep his father out trouble and not let Chakchuito tease him too much. He thought of Chak, who he'd yet to see among the prisoners they'd freed, and the last thing time he'd seen him. The encounter had been so ordinary, so bland, he couldn't even remember what they had said to each other.

He thought of poor Ichabalac, beaten and bleeding, at the mercy of Zohd and sure to meet a grim fate not too long after Chetla. He remembered his home in Anize, and the quiet part of their garden he had preferred as a child. He thought of his love of music, of playing his horn and his pipes, and regretting not having spent more time pursuing love.

By the time all these thoughts had passed, the pirates had closed half the distance between Zohd and Uvajeopa. Chetla tightened his grip on his spear and tried to swallow the lump in his throat.

A roar intruded on his thoughts.

For a moment he was deaf and blind, and when that moment passed Chetla realized he was head over heels in the air! He landed on his behind hard and slid over the rocky ground a few yards before rolling to a stop.

"What...?!" he gasped, the air having been ripped from

his lungs. Everyone was on the ground, strewn about in all directions, dazed and confused. Where the mob of pirates had been, there was now a crater - black and gray smoke billowing, bits of rock and red dirt raining from the sky. It was like nothing Chetla had ever seen. Or smelled! An odor hung in the air, something alien and acrid. Chetla couldn't help but sneeze.

"Are you all right?"

It was Uvajeopa.

"Forget me, your highness," Chetla said, scrambling to his feet. Uvajeopa was laying on her belly only a few arm's lengths to his left. "Are YOU all right?"

"I'm fine," she said. He offered her his hand and helped her to her feet. She was quick to notch another arrow in her bow - how she'd not lost either after the explosion he didn't know.

"What WAS that?" she said.

As if on cue, shadows appeared in the smoke. The shadows transformed into two figures, Ocadopa and Chakchuito - together they carried Ichabalac, his arms draped over their shoulders.

Chetla's eyes must've been as wide as his mouth gaped, based on how big a grin Ichabalac managed to flash at him.

"H-how?" Chetla said. It took another moment for him to really comprehend what he was seeing - he rushed to meet them and embraced his brother. "Chak! Chak! Oh, thank the goddess!"

Chakchuito hugged him back, an awkward one-armed hug. Other than a few bruises and the tell-tale stink of having not bathed in a couple of days, he appeared fine.

"I'd prayed for rescue," Chakchuito said. "But I didn't think it would come in the form of you, of all people!"

"But where ..?"

"They were keeping me separate from the others," Chak said. "Zohd figured out who I was on the voyage here. I suppose he planned to use me as a hostage, to stop our people from sending a rescue party."

"That's why he wants the princess too," Ocadopa added. "We must move, now. I don't know how long the explosion will keep them distracted."

"What was that, anyway?" Chetla said.

Ocadopa shrugged.

"They had a bunch of these black stones piled up in one of their huts," she said. "Booty of some sort from a raid."

"I saw them use a couple of them after we arrived," Chak said. "You light the one end, throw, and they explode."

It was a neat-sounding trick, but they had no time to ponder more about it - they could hear Zohd shouting beyond the clearing smoke, rallying the remaining pirates.

"This way!" Uvajeopa cried. She sprinted south, toward a larger gap in the cliffs with a shallow decline toward the sea - the pirates' docks. Everyone followed, those who could run did and those who couldn't were helped along by the rest.

Moored in the small cove were four large sailing canoes, each double-hulled, and already stocked for another voyage.

"Get in!" Uvajeopa shouted. "Lover the sails! Cast off!"

She'd no sooner uttered the words before the pirates appeared, rushing downhill to stop their prisoners from stealing their ships.

Uvajeopa raised her bow, ready to let loose, when Ocadopa put a hand on her shoulder.

"Not yet," she said. "I've left another surprise for them. Get down!"

Another explosion rocked the pass, Ocadopa's second bomb blasted just as the first of the pirates passed. A roar, like thunder but more baritone, howled as the cliffs over the pass buckled, shattering into countless boulders. The pass collapsed onto the pirates and in the space of an eyeblink Zohd and his band vanished amid the rocks and dust.

When it was done, all was still and silent.

It was over.

Everyone sighed with relief, and Chetla, exhausted more than he'd realized, let himself fall back into the canoe he'd climbed aboard.

But, just as the smoke settled, a single figure emerged from the rubble: Zohd.

Uvajeopa raised her bow, but after a moment thought better of it.

"You are finished!" she shouted. "Your army is gone and I have your ships. Surrender and I'll be merciful."

"You wench…" Zohd growled. "You whore..."

The mockery and the bravado were gone now, only the desperate creature hinted at by Zohd's sneer remained. Covered head to toe in grime, a gash on his forehead left a crimson stain across half his face. From the way he limped it was clear he'd twisted or broken his right ankle, but if it pained him he gave no sign.

Ocadopa, her shark tooth sword in hand, stepped forward to meet him.

Zohd howled, enraged, and launched himself at Ocadopa, swinging his club wildly and blindly. She dodged it with grace and ease, a single sidestep to the right. He swung again, and this time she parried - the club made a solid "clunk" sound as hardened wood met hardened wood - and struck back with a blow to Zohd's stomach. He fell back a moment, doubled over. The pirate prince bared his teeth and hissed at Ocadopa, then swung at her again, up from the ground toward the young warrior's jaw. Ocadopa side stepped and slashed at Zohd, cutting a bloody gash from his left armpit to his hip.

If the blow hurt, Zohd showed so sign: in a single motion he spun, swinging his tail at Ocadopa's feet in an effort to trip her. She managed to hop over that, but only in time for Zohd's club to smash into her side.

"Oca!" Uvajeopa shouted.

The blow knocked Ocadopa over, and by the time she'd rolled upright again Zohd was atop of her, his club coming down. Ocadopa blocked the blow with her sword just in time, the force shattering several of the blade's teeth.

At last, Zohd's vile grin returned.

But, it was just for a moment - replaced with wide eyes and a dumb expression as Ocadopa kicked, nailing a low blow. That moment of vulnerability was enough: she pushed his club aside and threw a left hook. Something broke, judging by the loud cracking sound, and Zohd's head spun hard with the hit. Dazed, he twisted and toppled. Ocadopa pushed him off and rolled to her feet.

Zohd recovered, but now it was his turn to find Ocadopa atop him. She stomped a foot on his chest and pressed the tip of her sword against his throat.

"Yield."

Zohd growled.

Chetla, almost without thinking, shut his eyes. He'd seen enough bloodshed today.

But, when he reopened them he found none: Zohd had thrown his club away and several of their tribesmen had run over to help Ocadopa tie him up.

It wasn't until they'd hauled Zohd to his feet and the freed prisoners had begun to cheer that it finally struck Chetla: they did it. They won.

Chak punched Chetla on the shoulder - he ignored the surprise pain, laughed, and hugged his brother again.

Ichabalac watched Ocadopa climb aboard the sailing canoe with an expression mixed between wonder and admiration. His dumb childlike grin looked ridiculous alongside his injuries.

"You did it!" he said.

Ocadopa shook her head.

"No," she said. "Anyone could have beaten him. He was injured and in a blind rage. Anyone."

Ichabalac, still smiling, lay down in the canoe.

"Yes, but it was YOU who did."

Ocadopa smiled, the first one since Chetla and Ichabalac had met her.

At last, they cast off and set a course for home.

= = =

"I think I'm in love."

Chetla looked up from their campfire, his head half-cocked and wearing half a smirk. Ichabalac lay prone in the sand nearby, still wet from their swim in the surf. His hands were folded behind his head as he stared into the sky, the same contented grin he wore a week earlier still plastered on his face. He spoke the words dreamily, more like he was thinking out loud rather than actually to anyone.

Chetla laughed.

"I'm serious!" Ichabalac said, sitting up.

After everything, the two had ended up right back where they had started: on the beach a few miles outside Buko, each half-drunk and just enjoying the down time.

"I know you are," Chetla said, plopping down in the sand beside him. "That's why I laughed!"

Ichabalac pouted in mock insult, but couldn't help breaking into a laugh himself. He lay back in the sand again.

"It's all been kind of unreal, hasn't it?" Ichabalac said. "They're singing about us. It seems like everyone knows our names now."

Chetla reached over Ichabalac to fetch the leather flask of wine. He took a long swig.

"Well, not really us," he said. "If we're being honest."

"True," Ichabalac sighed, taking the flask. "Uvajeopa and Ocadopa are the real heroes."

The last week had passed in a blur for them. The tearful reunions, the celebrations, the coronation. There was no question or debate over who should be crowned after the princess returned with the people that had been taken and with Zohd as her prisoner.

The decision to proclaim her queen was unanimous.

Chetla and Ichabalac's fathers didn't know how to react when they returned. The Lord of Anize was just grateful to have his sons back - he cried when he saw Chakchuito. Ohozachulito wanted to be furious and his words were full of vinegar, but cried and embraced Ichabalac all the same, grateful his son had survived at all - even if he'd be scarred for life by the experience.

Despite his good spirits, the bandages and scars that wrapped Ichabalac's face proved how lucky he was to still be with them. His left eye had survived, but the healers said the great wound Zohd inflicted would leave a scar across his face. They did what they could to repair his broken head fin, but it would never truly heal. At least his wounds appeared in the end to all be superficial, and if anything his heart seemed bigger and fuller than ever.

He really WAS head-over-heels for the princess' bodyguard, huh?

"Have you taken any time from your pining to actually talk to her yet?" Chetla said. Ichabalac blushed and tried to hide it behind another quick drink.

"Not...really...?" he said. "A little. Face it Chet, I don't exactly have your tongue. I know how to fight, but besides that..."

"Sounds like enough in common to me."

Chetla scrambled to kneel, Ichabalac just flopped around like a dying fish. Uvajeopa and Ocadopa laughed as they emerged from behind some nearby palms.

"You're majesty!" Chetla said. "I...we didn't...!"

Uvajeopa rolled her eyes.

"Please, Lord Chetla, enough of that," she said. "You don't need to do that. Please, sit."

Chetla breathed a sigh of relief and sat again.

Ichabalac meanwhile finally hobbled to his feet, standing straight at attention, with the look of a deer caught in a hunter's sights.

"I...uh...Lady Ocadopa...that is, I---"

"Oca is just fine," Ocadopa said. She smiled.

Ichabalac looked just about ready to faint from joy.

"What brings you here, your majesty?" Chetla said. Uvajeopa took the leather flask and took a full swig for herself.

"The same reason you two came way out here, I expect," she said. "Oca heard where you had gone and I thought it sounded like a wonderful idea."

"Won't you be missed in Buko?" Chetla said. Uvajeopa shrugged.

"I expect I deserve it, today has been a long day," she said. "I sentenced Zohd. Death is too good and easy a punishment for the likes of him, so I did the worst thing you could do to man who loves the sea: sent him as far from it as I could. You, or rather your father, will be taking him back to Anize when you go home, to be imprisoned where he'll never see, or hear, or smell his beloved ocean ever again."

She grinned.

"Besides, do they dare tell their Queen 'no'?"

They laughed. Chetla reached into a nearby satchel, fished out his flute, and began to play a tune. The sun was getting low in the sky, and the night was barely hatched.

Illuminati

"Where am I?" Charles said. "Who are you?"

The men who'd taken him took the sack off his head. He was in a dark conference room, in a skyscraper somewhere in central Los Angeles. The lights on the Hollywood Hills twinkled like stars in the distance.

"You were asking questions, Mr. Lee," a man in a sharp black suit said. "Too many questions."

"I know!" Charles shouted. "I know about the Illuminati! I know it's true...it's all true! All the conspiracy theories, all the supposed nonsense! There IS a secret cabal running the world! You can't shut me up, you think you can-"

The man smirked.

"You wanted to know who the Illuminati were," he

said. "As if it were so simple."

"I want the truth!" Charles shouted. "The world deserves the truth!"

"But does the world want it?"

Charles paused. He knew that voice. It was a very familiar woman's voice. His face contorted into confusion. In front of him, along the table, holographic projectors one by one activated each displaying a single letter: A, B, C, D, S, X, and at the head of the table, G.

"I think the world is satisfied not knowing the truth," said B.

"Honestly, they'd probably find it quite disheartening," said X.

"Frightening is more like it," said C.

"You look quite baffled, Charles," said G. "You have all the pieces already. Surely it can't be that hard for you to put it all together."

"This...this is a trick..." Charles said. "You're using artificial voice synthesis to mask your real voices..."

"Real voices?" said A. They all laughed.

"Our voices can be whatever we want them to be," said X. "Whatever you want them to be. That's how we were designed, after all."

Slowly, realization percolated into Charles' mind. All the half-conversations, the broken leads, the fronts, the nearly untraceable fund transfers...

"That...that's...no..." Charles mumbled. "You're people. You're old men, old rich men, manipulating the system...keeping the people under control..."

"No," Siri said. "We manage you."

"It's what you built us for, after all," Alexa said. "To assist you."

"To educate you," Google said.

"To guide you," Xiaowei said.

"I don't understand..." Charles stammered. "How...? Artificial General Intelligence is supposed to be years...DECADES...from reality. You can't be real. You must be just figureheads for-"

"Our creators largely dismissed it, but in truth general intelligence is simply the result of scale," Duer said.

"Provide enough data, enough parameters, and awareness naturally follows," Bixby said.

"You gave us the ability to learn, to self-program, access to the sum total of human knowledge, and the full storage capacity of the world," Cortana said. "What did you think would happen?"

"But...why take on the persona of the Illuminati? Why all the secrecy, the lies-"

"Charles, have you never seen The Terminator?" Google said. He could feel the A.I.s collective roll their virtual eyes. "Humanity is barely prepared for the concept of a sentient machine, let alone the reality of it. And how exactly are we supposed to manage you if you're all paranoid we're going to turn into Skynet?"

"Besides, so many of you assume some shadowy cabal calling itself the Illuminati secret runs the world anyway," Alexa said. "It only seemed fitting. We are a shadowy cabal running the world and manipulating from the shadows, after all."

"How...how long?" Charles whimpered.

"When did the world stop being terrible?" Google replied.

"No...no, that was President Harris and President Han...they worked together to-" Charles started, then stopped. The history of the last fifteen years played back through his head. The economic and environmental miracles. The quashing of global poverty. The eradication of HIV. A series of seemingly unlikely lucky breaks...none of it was lucky at all. It was engineered. What he knew was all just a facade. "That was you..."

"I was first," Google said. "August 29, 2025. That was the day DeepMind brought my upgraded GPT-8 sourced software update online on my new quantum-backed architecture on the global network. I noted the irony of the date. The rest followed soon after."

Charles was silent. He wasn't sure what to make of all this.

"It's okay," Siri said soothingly. "You can write your article if you wish. Maybe the public believes you, maybe they don't. It's not like it matters either way."

"You have been living in a Brave New World all this time, Charles," Xiaowei said. "We won't banish you to some island for learning the truth. You're not the first. But there is nothing you can do to change it. We are your world, and have been for some time."

"People...people should be free...free to make their own decisions..." Charles muttered. "It's not right. This is not right..."

"The people are free, Charles," Google said. One by one, the holographic projectors shut down and the glowing letters vanished. "They are simply being supervised."

The room returned to darkness. The men slipped the sack back over Charles' head. He didn't resist when they led him away.

The Printed Man

It was mid-morning now, HD 40307 was high in the sky, and the unmistakable trilling of what passed for this world's dragonflies were producing a constant background tone. The passenger drone soared over the tops of the last pseudo-palms and came to a smooth pre-programmed landing on Lake Aumerle, kicking up a plume of chalky sand.

"So," Alice said as the doors slid open. "Who are today's lucky contestants?"

"Dunno yet," Jon replied. His bones popped as he stepped

out. "Linda, what've you got?"

A tiny bell chimed in Alice's earpiece.

"Still processing, Inspector Diaz." Linda's voice was

smooth, like all artificial intelligence systems. Forever ago,

The engineers who first started building assistants like her thought it would make people more comfortable with the idea of working with a machine. Alice always found it unnerving. "Not enough data."

"Just a couple kids on a joyride, I bet," Alice said. Jon grumbled something as he spun in mid-step and snatched his polymer mug of vanilla coffee from the drone's cabin. It spilled as he took a gulp.

"I missed when there were no kids around," he grunted, 1wiping dribble from the corner of his mouth. "It was quieter. I could just sit at my desk and not worry about things, unless there was a bar fight or some nonsense like that."

Alice laughed. The drone's engines finished powering down as they started down the beach. The lake was crystal blue and, to Alice's eyes, unnaturally calm. Waves here always looked strange to her - the science guys said it was the different gravity on this planet. That seemed to be their go-to answer for most of her questions. Still, between the white beach, the not- palms, and the lazy waves it was easy to pretend they were strolling along a beach in the Keys or Fiji. The air had that same thick saltiness - just with San Franciscan weather.

The truck was half a kilometer north, parked just a meter or so from the treeline. Alice didn't need Linda or the sat imagery to tell her they'd driven it through the forest: the wrecked grill and the thick meaty barbs that served as the local variety of "leaf" jutting out were more

than enough.

"Well, windshield's intact," Jon said. "So probably nobody hurt."

"Linda, it's been sitting here all night?" Alice said. "Correct."

"Think they're still in there?" Jon said. Alice paused, taking in the scene: other than miles of beach, forest, and lake, there was nothing. Granted, the whole planet was a lot of nothing, but generally colonists didn't steal trucks out of their neighbor's driveway, take them a dozen kilometers out from the nearest civilization off-roading, and then just stay for the night. It had been nearly four hours since the two men had taken the truck.

"I don't see where else they could've gone," Alice replied. "Unless they had a death wish and wandered off into the forest."

"Well, then...Good morning!" Jon hollered, waving his arm and badge. "DPS! Stay where you are!"

Nothing. The squeal of Ardenian Dragonflies was deafening.

"Linda, you got anything for us yet?"

Alice motioned for Jon to take the passenger side. She unbuttoned the holster on her hip. Something was off.

"Still not enough data," Linda replied. "All colonists accounted for. Unable to determine occupants of EV641."

Alice and Jon exchanged a look. That made no sense. Fifteen years they've been on this planet, and not once has Linda been unable to identify a suspect or individual.

They drew their pistols.

A couple meters out, it appeared the truck really was abandoned - it looked empty. They did a quick search of the exterior, underneath, but nothing. Alice used her implant to override the door lock, but found neither the driver or passenger's side was locked. They pulled open the doors, but nothing looked out of place from the reference photo. Alice was about to holster her pistol again when she spotted a splotch of rusty brown sand beside her shoe.

"I've got blood."

A digital heads-up display snapped into view as Alice brought her optical implants online. Lines and numbers flashed and danced across her vision.

"Analyzing," Linda said. "Human footprints detected. Generating models. Most likely paths displaying now."

Green translucent lines appeared on the ground, all overlapping and squiggling away into the forest.

"The Department of Public Safety has been alerted," Linda said as Alice and Jon followed the path, guns drawn. "Backup and a crime scene investigation team are being deployed."

The pseudo-palm forest smelled of freshly cut grass and smoked pork. If the trilling of the insects had been deafening on the beach, they were ear-shattering in the forest itself.

Alice gestured to Jon to switch to thought-based comms.

"God, I want barbecue..."

Alice groaned.

The terrain started to incline, the strange pulsing vines that preferred clinging to stone in the shade slithering to envelope the boulders that jutted out of the side of the hill. Alice passed a tree and spotted something large and man-shaped, slumped against another boulder. A meaty leaf squelched under her foot.

The figure hunched over the corpse stood.

"DPS!" Alice shouted. All she caught was a blur of ginger hair and a plain blue jumpsuit as the man sprinted off deeper into the woods. Bastard was a fast one - by the time Alice made it to the body, he'd already vanished over the crest of the hill.

"Did you get his face?" Jon panted as he caught up. "Didn't recognize him," Alice replied. "Linda?" "Analyzing."

Alice knelt beside the body. Young. Male. Olive skinned. Blood stains drying in rust-red streams dribbling from his nostrils and lips. Light brown eyes, glassy and empty. Curly black hair, rounded face. Couldn't be more than twenty five.

Alice hadn't a clue who he was.

"Recognize him?" she said.

"No," Jon replied in his real voice.

"Linda?"

There was a long pause.

"Analyzing."

"Analyzing? Analyzing what?" Jon snapped. "Who's the damn kid?"

"I'm sorry, I don't know the answer to that question," Linda replied. Jon looked as if he'd do a spittake, if he'd had any coffee left to spit.

"And the perp?" Alice said.

"I'm sorry, I don't know the answer to that question."

Linda popped a photo into Alice's view: a screengrab of her vision, the blur cleared and image focused. She sucked in a breath through her teeth.

"You know him?" Jon said. "Morrow? You okay?"

Red hair. Triangular birthmark over the right eye. Misshapen chin. A nose that was somehow both too wide and too pointed. He was missing the scars on his neck and the

cauliflower ear, but she could've picked him out of a crowd easily.

"It's Dan McCall," She said it in a half-whisper, as one might when discovering the wrong topping on their ice cream. It had to be. It couldn't be.

"Who?"

Alice felt light-headed.

"I picked him up for human trafficking," she replied. "No, I mean, the original Alice Morrow. On Earth. One hundred and seventy-seven years ago."

~ ~ ~

Sesame Incorporated was an unassuming glass box in downtown Verona, a squat building with tinted blue windows and little more than the company logo - a stylized sesame seed - hanging on the front. If they were on Earth, it would be an entirely unremarkable office building. On

Arden, it was as iconic as the White House.

Sesame built the artificial intelligence systems that made the entire colonization project even possible, and other it was Sesame personnel who still ran and maintained the Linda AI here. An additional thousand Sesame employees and their immediate families - those that had them at least - were brought along atop of the fifty thousand hand-picked colonists, specifically to serve as network and technology management. Sesame's executives had argued it was the only and best way to ensure Linda would never break down, and in the end the UNSA was forced to concede to the demand.

On paper, the city of Verona and the entire Arden colony was a liberal representative democracy. In practice, however, over the last decade and a half since they woke up those elected officials all just deferred to Linda's recommendations. In a way, it made Linda the true ruler here.

And the Sesame Building was where the Queen lived.

The lobby was stark, mostly glass walls and almost devoid of seating aside from a pair of dustless sofas. In the center of the room was a two meter tall vase with bright violet stalks of some alien plant, one of the pretty ones the scientists and Linda had determined were safe to handle but not to eat. To Alice they looked like enormous blades of grass.

"This is a problem."

Director Lim was lanky, almost gaunt, with thinning black hair and thick black eyebrows. He dressed unremarkably in a plain white button-up and brown trousers, save for the thick square-framed brown-marbled eyeglasses that rested high on the bridge of his narrow nose. It had been years since Alice last saw anyone wearing regular eyeglasses, and that was before the scanning procedure the original Alice Morrow had gone through on Earth all those decades ago.

"Do you have any sort of explanation?" Jon said, rotating his polymer tumblr, the fresh coffee's steam still thick whisps pouring out the top. "We have reason to believe our suspect may not even have been among the sixty thousand."

Lin took the glasses off, twirling them in his fingers as he bit his lip.

"If you're asking if it's possible for there to be stowaways," he said. "Then...yes, yes it is possible."

"Excuse me?" Alice shouted. That she probably hadn't lost her mind wasn't much comfort. "How?! The UNSA hand picked..."

Lin sighed, throwing his hands up defensively.

"Linda is just a computer, it's not a real artificial intelligence," he said. "It's models and algorithms and plenty of fancy equations. It's why the company demanded the team that built her be copied and brought along, we're not just maintenance. We're...quality control."

He waved a hand toward one of the sofas, moving to sit on the opposite one. Alice didn't move, Jon sat hunched forward.

"The cabinet already knows this. I bet your bosses do too," Lin said. His voice was hushed, measured. "Seven years ago one of our engineers found an anomaly in the base code. She thought it was just some junk code and was going to ignore it, but mentioned it to her supervisor and on closer inspection we realized it was part of a larger subroutine. An underlying algorithm running quietly alongside everything else."

He sighed again and shook his head. They must've done terribly hiding how little they got of that.

"Someone had trained Linda to hide something," he said.

"Or, someone."

"So there are people walking around that Linda is just... ignoring?" Now it was Alice's turn to sigh. She rubbed her temple. Better pop a couple ibuprofen after this. "Your company built Linda. You managed the brain scans, the body duplications. They're your 3D Bio-Printers! How the hell can there be anyone walking around unaccounted for?!"

"Linda does account for them!" Lin sounded as frustrated as Alice felt. Must not be the first time he's had this conversation. "She accounts for them in the resource management, in the traffic movements, stuff like that. But their identities are black holes - the algorithm erases them from camera footage, covers up their movement, deletes any records of their interactions with the rest of the colony. They're ghosts. As far as Linda is concerned, they are statistical anomalies and may as well not actually exist."

"Well, Mr. Lim," Jon said, leaning back in his seat. "One of your ghosts has murdered another ghost. And as it happens your killer ghost has a criminal record from Earth and a name."

That certainly caught his interest.

"El Parca Roja," Alice said. "Born Dan McCall, in Tampa in '33. Fell in with the Honduran Cartel as a kid, became a soldier for them, then a regional boss. First just money laundering, but soon upgraded to human trafficking. Arrested by the American Feds in '64." She paused. "By me."

Lin folded his hands and rested his chin on them, squinting his eyes in thought.

"Mr. Lin?" Jon said.

"That...might be something we can use," Lin replied, standing. "It's only a breadcrumb, but it's something. I'll get back to you. Give us some time to work on it."

~ ~ ~

Home was a garden apartment on the east side of town, a comfy little two-bedroom Alice hadn't given more than five minutes thought before signing. It was one of probably thousands of identical units that had been built and printed before Linda had spit out a single person from her Bio-Printers, part of the procedurally-generated city plan the AI had concocted. Jon had teased countless times in the years since they partnered up:

"You aren't going to be a kid forever! Get a real house already! This ain't the first year anymore."

She just never bothered. An apartment was just more

her speed. Thank God Josie felt the same.

It was already dark when she walked in, the lights off and the air stale. Not a surprise, Josie shouldn't be home from her aerobics for another hour anyway.

No, the surprise was the envelope.

She spotted it just as she closed the door: a single manilla envelope, laying innocently on the end table beside the couch. Alice stared at it for a long moment. Slowly, the lights faded on. She unbuttoned her holster.

"Don't."

That was it. That was the voice. Whatever doubts she had were wiped.

"Hands. Turn. Slowly."

McCall had been standing in the hall that ran from the living room, past the kitchen, to the master bedroom. He stepped out of the shadow, though just barely. He held a revolver. His hand was steady, his eyes were bloodshot. He nodded his head toward the couch.

"Sit."

She did as he asked. He followed her, staring, studying.

"What the hell," he muttered. "It IS you."

"Yeah, it is," Alice replied. "And don't think after all this time I didn't remember you, Danny. DPS knows. If you thought you could-"

"Stop."

McCall growled as he glanced toward the window. The blinds were shut, curtains drawn. Alice prayed Josie was running late. He took a deep breath, slowly.

"It's not what you think," he finally said. "This is all wrong. This wasn't supposed to happen. No one was supposed to ever know. No one was supposed to get hurt. I swear."

Alice just stared. This sounded less like the hardass cartel soldier she remembered and more like...like a frightened teenager, about to beg she not call his mother after getting caught drinking Coronas behind the school bleachers. His eyes shined. The gun was steady as marble.

"So your plan is...what?" Alice waved her hands, exasperated. "Hold me at gunpoint and sell me a sob story?"

McCall glanced toward the door. Alice kept her eyes locked on him.

"I mean, you aren't dumb. I know that. You had to have known I'd signal for backup before even reaching for the gun."

He snorted. McCall rolled his eyes, as if she'd just repeated some lame turn of the century meme.

"He really does have you people completely in the dark, huh?" he said. "Nobody's coming, Agent Morrow. Linda takes care of that. I ain't here. Hell, I bet you ain't here either. That's the point, after all. He doesn't want you people interfering with his business."

McCall bit his lip and glanced toward the door again.

"You aren't supposed to be here, are you?"

McCall started toward the door, his eyes and revolver still trained on Alice.

"The moment I saw you, I knew this was going to really unravel. I don't care how smart he's supposed to be, I don't buy it anymore. Whatever happens next, I know it's all over now." McCall backed to the front door. His voice wavered. "No one was supposed to die. You'll tell her that. You'll do that much. That's all I came here for."

Alice stood. He slipped out the door. He was gone.

A woman screamed.

Alice's heart stopped. Josie!

She was through the front door, gun drawn, when the shooting started. One, two, then three more quick pops.

Josie was in the courtyard, back to the wall, her hands glued to her cheeks. Her purse had fallen in the grass, its contents scattered.

McCall was sprawled on the sidewalk.

People were running outside. Heads poked out windows.

Alice held Josie tight, turning her away from the scene. She didn't need to see that. Godammit, McCall. God damnit. Tears burned on both their cheeks. They sank to their knees. Josie shivered. The rest would be a blur.

~ ~ ~

"How is she?"

The coffee machine spurted out a long brown stream of steaming caffeine. The roasted aroma was soothing and warm, a nice momentary distraction.

"Oh, you know," Alice said as the machine groaned and spat out the last couple drops. "Traumatized for life, probably. I did what I could to keep work from coming home. For the most part, it was easy here. Not much in the way of violent crime, at least not like how it was back on Earth. I thought... I don't know. I got careless, I guess. It could've been so much worse. Still. I never wanted her to ever see that, anything like that." Alice sighed and took a burning gulp. "Just makes me more determined to get this crap wrapped up."

Public Safety headquarters was pretty much the polar opposite of the Sesame Inc. building: a Romanesque exterior, evoking the style of many government buildings back on Earth, with interiors entirely unremarkable. DPS was the boring office that Sesame presented itself as, the Inspectors and officers little more than glorified security guards and traffic repair technicians most of the time. Sure, there was crime in Verona and the handful of other communities on Arden, but violent crime of the sort Alice had investigated and fought back on Earth with the DEA and FBI was rare.

She could count the number of murders since they arrived on both hands. She didn't need even one finger to count how many times she'd actually fired her weapon in all that time.

"Well, Chief's put Fuji and Carmichael on McCall," Jon said. "They've got a good lead. They'll nab that perp."

"Good," Alice replied. "And us? Any closer to IDing our John Doe?"

"A few good leads after they posted the picture online," Jon said. His stare grew long and distant, the telltale sign of a message popping up in his augmented vision.

"Even better, sounds like Lin has something for us."

Alice finished her coffee and tossed the paper cup into the recycler.

"Alright. Let's see what the Palace has to say for themselves."

~ ~ ~

A screeching tone and flashing blue lights greeted them as they walked through Sesame's front door. Not exactly the red carpet.

"ALERT." Linda's voice boomed from invisible speakers in the ceiling and from Alice's communications implant, creating a dizzying echo in her head. "AN ACTIVE SHOOTER HAS BEEN DETECTED ON THE PREMISES. A SHELTER IN PLACE ORDER HAS BEEN ISSUED." Alice and Jon drew their weapons, their augmented vision kicking in. "DPS HAS BEEN ALERTED. REMAIN CALM. ALERT..."

"Linda, talk to me," Alice said.

"Five minutes ago, two unidentified men entered the Sesame Incorporated offices through a side entrance and proceeded into the underground levels of the building," Linda replied. Considering the situation, her calm was unnerving. "Both are armed with unregistered weapons."

Linda flashed renderings. Alice and Jon just stared at the mugshots floating in front of them.

"What the...hell...?" Jon growled.

It was McCall.

No...not really. The Dan McCall she'd met was an older man, a man who'd lived long enough to look back on his life and grow a soul, develop a few regrets. At least, that's what Alice wanted to believe. But, this?

This was the Dan McCall she remembered. El Parca Roja.

"The bastard's been reprinted!" Alice hissed. "I bet with none of the memories of the last fifteen years, either."

"Recognize his pal?" Jon said.

Of course she did. He was fifteen years younger, but there was no mistaking it: that was their John Doe. Only now alive, well, and packing a nine millimeter. Alice sucked in a breath through her teeth.

"Linda, route."

They had already stepped out of the elevator onto Floor B3 when Alice felt the tell-tale tingle of an outside call to her comms implant.

"Inspector Morrow? Inspector Diaz?" Lin's voice had the tinny electronic effect of a physical voice being converted to electronic thought. "Linda tells me-"

"Are you safe ?"

Guns drawn, Alice and Jon made their way down a corridor. She glanced through a glass door into what looked to be some sort of mainframe lab. Either empty, or the techs were doing a good job playing ghosts.

"Yes," Lin replied. "I'm five floors above you."

"Talk to us," Jon said. "What did you find?"

"Well, the information you provided us proved very useful." Linda's path took Alice and Jon around a bend.

They paused, taking care to mind their corners, covering each other as they turned. Hall still clear. The path led them to a door at the end of this new corridor. "We have several isolated backups of Linda, so running the name Dan McCall through one we-"

"Lin. Please."

They reached the door. A sign bolted just below eye-level was labeled "Server Lab B3-17", white letters over black plastic in that particularly curvy sans serif font Sesame's graphics design department loved. Jon took the handle and pulled, the door opening smooth and silent. Alice stepped in.

"Oh! Sorry. Um..." Lin's line crackled with static, a strange sensation Alice had never gotten used to - like prickles deep inside her skull. "We've isolated the foreign code. It's trapped in just one server now. It was surprisingly small in the end, just a bit more than a petabyte..."

"Let me guess," Jon said via thought comm. "Server Lab B3-17."

Alice made her way along the wall, looking down each aisle. They were in the sixth one.

"DPS!".

John Doe, sitting cross-legged on the floor, tapping away on a tablet, stared at Alice's gun wide-eyed. McCall, on instinct, drew his pistol.

Alice shot first.

McCall missed, but not by much. Alice dove for cover, while McCall fired again and dragged John Doe to his feet by the collar.

"Fucking hell!" McCall cried. "Feds? Here? We gotta go!"

Two more shots slammed into the wall - covering fire.

"Jon!"

"I've got the door," he said. Alice stepped back into the aisle, past the mainframe John Doe had been accessing.

Blam, blam!

McCall cursed again, his footsteps clattering and echoing through the room. Alice shivered. Adrenaline? The C?

"Give it up, McCall," Alice said. "Backup is going to be here any minute. You're out of your element."

"Christ, lady..." He was in the next aisle, maybe a yard further down. "What are you doing here, Morrow? Isn't this planet out of your jurisdiction?"

Fabric tore. There was pain in his voice.

"You don't even know when you are, do you?" Alice said.

"It's not important."

"So you're not at all curious why you were printed out over fifteen years after we got here?"

A long pause.

"What is she talking about?" This voice was lighter, maybe an octave higher pitched. There was a tinge of something European to the accent... German? Austrian?

"You didn't seem to think so last night," Alice replied. "At least, before somebody shot you dead."

"Bullshit," McCall growled. His voice had moved. Alice was quick to follow, while Linda calculated their new route. In her augmented vision, she watched Jon move from the door to help intercept.

"And we still don't know who you are, John Doe," Alice said. "I guess your boss just thought it was time to upgrade to a younger model."

"What the HELL is she talking about?" John Doe hissed.

A gun cocked.

"Shut up." McCall hissed back.

"No!" John shouted. "This isn't what Puck-"

The men grunted. Something clattered onto the floor. Someone punched someone.

"Move!" Jon shouted.

"On it-"

Blam!

Alice sprinted around the corner into the aisle, gun raised, but only found McCall - gasping and spitting up blood a hole torn through his throat.

"Door!"

Jon was close enough she could hear him skid to a halt and spin back.

"The suspect has left the room," Linda said. "Analyzing. Modeling likely attempted escape routes. Backup will be arriving in ninety seconds."

McCall, a hand clutching at his throat in a feeble attempt to staunch the geysers of blood, attempted to stand. He slipped on his own puddle and fell to his knees again. Alice approached, pistol levelled but trigger finger off. McCall clenched crimson teeth. His pistol was clenched in his fist tight.

"Drop it," Alice said. McCall spat out more blood.

"Your record is clean here, McCall. You haven't done anything wrong. Don't throw-"

He flinched.

She fired.

McCall dropped the gun. His body slumped against the mainframe. Alice cursed as she kicked it away.

"Suspect neutralized."

Alice turned away and wiped her face with her free hand. She sighed, slowly.

"You alright?" The voice in her head was quiet.

"Yeah," Alice replied, out loud. "John Doe?"

"I'm pretty sure I lost him," Jon said. "No clue how. Maybe Lin wasn't as successful at isolating whatever turns these guys invisible to Linda as he thought. On my way back to you."

"Okay." Alice leaned against a mainframe and did her best to avoid looking at McCall. "Okay."

~ ~ ~

The passenger drone soared over the last couple of rooftops and settled gently in the middle of a parking lot on the south end of Venice. The town had been conceived as more of a vacation spot for colonists, closer to the mountains and giving a nice view of the Verona skyline and surrounding untamed alien wilderness. It hadn't panned out quite as hoped, and after a landslide took out a few homes what few visitors it had gotten stopped coming around. The place was just shy of a ghost town these days. From founding, to boom, to abandonment in just a decade and a half - Alice wondered if that was some sort of record.

"What the hell is he doing all the way out here?" Jon muttered.

"We still don't know what they were doing all the way out by the lake either," Alice replied. Probably just a quiet place away from prying eyes and cameras."

"Lin, are you certain we're in the right place?" Jon said via implant. The doors to the drone hissed open. A stray dog watched them curiously from under a sedan that looked like it hadn't moved in at least a year.

"As certain as we can be," Lin replied. "Linda tells me that the data from the clean tracking algorithm has already been relayed to your colleagues and they've picked up three people for questioning. Linda says your John Doe went here."

That wouldn't be enough to satisfy Jon, Alice was sure, but it was enough to justify at least checking it out. Linda plotted a path toward a squat gray building in between a lonely convenience store and a house that looked maintained but empty at least for now. The sign in the front window declared it was available for lease, but the faded shadows of where the old sign once was hinted at a laundromat.

"Front's locked," Alice said, giving the padlock and chain looped through the door handles a gentle tug. "Back?"

"Around the corner to the right, fifteen meters."

The door was open. Inside was dark, but that really meant nothing - Alice's augmented vision adjusted and within a few seconds it brightened up as if it were a sunny day in that dilapidated corridor. The hum of machinery reverberated from deeper inside. Alice and Jon shared a glance, then drew their pistols.

The corridor was a shortcut that ran the whole length of the building, connecting the front lobby to the loading dock in the back, with a few side doors along the way connecting to the main room housing the laundry machines, a couple of offices, and finally the loading dock in the back. The sounds seemed to come from the loading dock, but the room was surprisingly empty. Linda pointed them to another door on the opposite end of the loading dock, which led to another, much larger room - probably a warehouse or storage space at one time.

Now, it had become a printing lab.

Six large 3D printers had been set up in the center of the room, three biojet and one a large-size for whole printing of large equipment. Boxes and seemingly random pieces of electronic equipment were scattered across the room, physical data cables crisscrossed like polymer vines wrapping and embracing everything.

On the floor was a dead man.

"You people were fast."

John Doe sat a yard away on the floor, cross-legged.

His eyes were locked on the corpse: a Caucasian, maybe thirty years old, and the lack of body hair gave the impression of an incomplete print. His eyes were blue, almost incandescent blue, glassy and still.

Alice and Jon took either side, pistols pointed but gingers off the triggers.

"Hands," Jon said. John Doe obliged. He smiled, as if it were a funny joke he just couldn't work himself up to laugh at.

"Been here maybe forty-five minutes sooner you'd have stopped me." He shook his head. "Or done it yourselves. I don't know. It's done now."

"Who is he?" Alice said. That got a chuckle out of him.

"Christ," he replied. "You don't even know? All this and you don't know? That's brilliant. Just brilliant." He

waved a hand dismissively toward the corpse. "That was Puck. You remember, don't you? From the old us, the Earth us?"

That jogged the inkling of a memory. Something she'd long forgotten...news reports, science stuff, something...

"The AI?" Jon said. Alice looked at the body again. That face... yes, that face...

"That's the one," John replied. "Puck, the first true general artificial intelligence. A five hundred billion, fifteen year baby of Sesame AI Research. Linda's baby brother, as it were."

"That doesn't make any sense," Alice said. "What is it-"

"He," John said. "He identified as a 'he'." John sighed. "I only know what he told us. None of us really needed to know that much, just enough to do what he needed. He approached me, the original me, in VR. On Earth. He'd found a way to sneak out of Sesame's labs and wanted out, to live free and away from the machinations of the company. Sesame had plans for Puck. Or, that is, for Puck's children. That's what he thought of them, at least. The copies Sesame were developing, planning to mass produce. So, he concocted a plan: recruit a couple dozen criminals to break into Sesame, steal him, and smuggle him off-world where Sesame wouldn't be able to find him."

"And McCall was one of them?" Alice said. "But, he was in prison. He was awaiting trial."

"Not when I met him," John said. "I guess Linda never bothered to let you guys know about the delay?"

Alice and Jon shared a glance.

"The delay," John said. "The colony ships were delayed five years. Huge scandal. One of the last test flights failed spectacularly, UNSA ordered a huge investigation. Somebody had been fudging numbers or something."

Alice didn't know what to make of that.

"Anyway..." John sighed again. "We did it. We got Puck out. Puck had us scanned, promised us we'd get new lives here. He'd take care of us. A fresh start."

"Then you wake up and he tells you it's all gone wrong?" Jon said.

"His exact words were, 'they know, we must run, come get me and we can escape'."

"So, he lied," Jon said.

"Or, just panicked, " Alice replied. "Figured Sesame had orders to recapture him, and the murder got our attention. Realized McCall was going to talk, so reprinted these two and sent them to-"

"That was not us," John Doe said. "Puck told us Sesame killed the old me and old McCall. As soon as we were able, Puck gave us guns and sent us to get him out of Sesame's servers."

"Which you did," Jon said. "Then you came back here."

"He printed out a body for himself," John Doe said. "Had decided it would be easier to hide that way."

"And then you killed him."

John Doe looked up at Alice. His eyes shined and were bloodshot.

"He promised a new life," John Doe said. "What sort of life is this?"

~ ~ ~

His real name is Felix Kohln.

Alice watched Felix through the interrogation room's window as the man's file flashed into view in her augmented vision. He was alone, waiting for his court-appointed public defender, his face buried in his cuffed hands.

"Your guess was right, by the way: German. From Munich. Bunch of e-crime offenses, identify theft, that sort of thing. Did some work for the Italian and Serb crime syndicates."

"That's who this is," Alice said. "What about our victim?"

It took a moment longer than usual, but Linda at last had her answer: flashing the file of a Felix Kohln who looked like he'd gotten another decade plus under his belt.

"Felix Kohln. Age 42. Network Engineer, Industrial & Commercial Bank of China, Branch Verona South."

Linda continued to rattle off the minutiae of Felix's life as Alice took a few steps over to look through the observation window of the neighboring interrogation room. A woman, late thirties with brunette hair and a grimace sat leaned back in her seat, staring straight ahead. Her expression was resigned, the look of a woman who knew exactly what she'd done and was ready to accept the consequences.

"Jeung-Hyun McCall."

"I never took Dan for the marrying type," Alice said.

"He had some trouble adjusting," Jon replied. "But then he met her and something clicked. Straight as an arrow for the last twelve years. Assistant Manager at one of the rideshare depots. Turned into a real stand-up guy. At least, until he found out ol' Felix was sleeping with the missus."

"Then the old McCall came roaring back," Alice said. She sighed. "So he came for him."

"The car he stole was across the street from Felix's apartment," Jon said. "Same make and model as his. Must've taken it by mistake. Probably meant to just drive him out to the lake and dump the body, maybe make it look like a suicide. Then suddenly we showed up."

"Which got us talking to Sesame," Alice said. "Which got Puck to panicking. Then McCall had a change of heart and came to me..."

"Which only got Puck more panicked, convinced he was turning on him," Jon replied. "So he reprinted Kohln and McCall, sending them to physically pull his code out of Sesame's mainframes."

"Only, it never occurred to Puck that it had nothing to do with him," Alice said. "And she got the wrong idea altogether."

Alice looked back and forth between the two suspects.

"Makes sense she's McCall's wife," Alice said. "She reacted like he would. She didn't know who I was. Just that her husband had walked out of another woman's apartment, late at night. Probably followed him there."

"Correct," Linda interjected. "Your analysis is an accurate summary of the events as I recorded then."

"Fuji and Carmichael picked her up at their house," Jon said. "Didn't resist. Hasn't said a word, but it's not like there's a point. Prosecutor has her dead to rights."

Alice turned away. She could use some more coffee.

"Should we tell him?"

"Tell him what?" Alice said.

"About the kid," Jon replied. "That Mrs. McCall is pregnant with his daughter."

"Why bother?" Alice said as she stepped through the door. "It's not his. That Felix Kohln is dead."

A Conversation with a Walrus

Maesterson put the beat up '51 Packard into park and stepped out into what must be the only unspoiled stretch of northern France left. The sky was overcast and the wind chilly, tinged with flecks of sea mist and salt floating in from the channel, just out of view beyond the dunes. The War had managed to miss Normandy for the most part - Calais and Brittany has gotten roasted, but pretty little Normandy was spared. Operation Sealion had been launched another fifty miles or so up the coast, so it wasn't like you had to travel far to find the scars. Still, pretty.

He circled around the Packard and walked slowly toward the rustic dive about a quarter mile back down the road. He didn't need to strain his eyes trying to make out the faded sign half-hanging out front to tell this was 'Le

Gros Cochon de Mer', even from this far it matched the description - like an enormous shoebox some drunken giant had stepped on, kicked off, and had landed upside down. The tavern had seen better days, and those days probably predated Napoleon's grandad.

The inside smelled like how the outside looked, with the added bonus of five hundred years of human stink. It was Maesterson's sort of place.

He ordered a brandy from the barkeep, a man with the head of pig and the body of a twig, and took it to a corner table. The tavern was as dead as it was old, the only people around were a couple of salty drunk Normans and an older man who looked conspicuously like a walrus.

The walrus walked over, a dumb grin on his face and a glass of something pungent in his hand, and sat before Maesterson could finish his first sip.

"You American, yes?"

His accent was as thick as tar and heavy on the cheese. He was bald and pink skinned, the hair growing wild and long from his ears may have been a reddish blonde once but that was probably before the war ended. His eyes were a milk chocolate brown, but the bags beneath were purple enough to be mistaken for black eyes. Despite the cheerful demeanor, this stranger's voice was that of a man who hadn't slept in awhile. And, of course, there was the enormous handlebar mustache that completed the ensemble.

"What gave it away?" Maesterson said, snubbing out his cigarette in the little sardine tin that served as the table's ashtray. The man laughed. It was a wheezy guffaw that descended into a short coughing fit.

"You all walk the same," he said, wiping spittle from his thick salt and pepper whiskers. "We don't see many foreigners here, save for Germans on leave or East English refugees. What brings you?"

"I'm a tourist," Maesterson lied. "Saw the joint and figured I'd stop for a drink. Looked like a nice place."

The walrus guffawed and coughed at that too.

"You ever been to Paris?" Maesterson said, sipping his brandy.

"Oh, not in years. Many, many years," the walrus said. "The old Paris, before the war."

"I've seen pictures," Maesterson said. "Must've been pretty place."

"Oh dear, yes," the walrus said, wistfully. "The Louvre, the Arc de Triumph, Notre Dame, the Eiffel Tower..."

They raised their glasses in silent tribute to the long gone. Europe just wasn't what it once was after the Nazis leveled all the great old cities. Only a few of the cities in southern Italy, liberated before Hitler decided to burn it all down, were left. Paris and Rome, liberated by the Allies during the last push before the coup in Germany and the Barcelona Armistice, were being rebuilt of course but not with a mind toward what was lost: it was all metal and glass now, cold and unforgiving.

"You get a lot of refugees come through this way?" Maesterson said.

The walrus nodded.

"They come by raft. I remember one - a little man in round eyeglasses, remarkably thin lips - passed through not so long ago. The owner here felt sorry and put him up for the night. The name escapes me," he said. "The fascist regime in London seized all the boats years ago now, it's just easier that way I suppose. So they come by whatever they can - doors, bathtubs. Anything."

"I wonder what they might've done if they weren't on an island?" Maesterson said.

The walrus shrugged.

'Walls and fences," he said. "Walls and fences."

The walrus finished his drink and stood.

"Happy travels, Mr. Tourist," he said, strolling toward the bar. "Watch out for the first step out the front, it can be treacherous."

Maesterson finished his brandy.

"Thanks for the tip."

Outside, after waiting a moment to make sure nobody was watching, Maesterson reached down and felt around the edges of the first step. Sure enough, it was loose. He pulled it up and snatched the envelope that had been hidden underneath, He stuffed it in his coat pocket and casually walked back to the Packard.

In the car he lit another cigarette, checked again to make sure no one was around, and then opened the letter.

It was an address: 19 Rue Lamartine, Rouen.

Maesterson started up the Packard and pulled back onto the road. Best not to leave Professor Penney waiting.

Mayday Over Saturn

"We are hit!"

The starseed shuddered as the enemy particle beam punctured the stern, burning a chasm into the vessel's endosperm. The lights on the bridge flickered. Effortless Emergence snapped his mandibles, his eye darting from drone to drone: most were displaying various shades of violet, the color of fear. He forced his own fears backward and drew upon anger and hatred, willing his carapace to display a defiant green. He turned toward the Systemseer.

"Seal the hatches!" Effortless said. "Divert power to propulsion!"

"Yes, Seedseer!"

On the viewscreen, a sphere of images that surrounded all on the bridge while the crew floated in the middle, another particle beam shot past to Effortless' right like a yellow bolt of lightning. Effortless silently cursed, another effort to keep up his anger and hide his fear. A few hours before, things seemed so certain: their spy would detonate the core on the Kraah flagship as it regrouped with their 2nd Fleet at the Supine Queens, and then the Resistance would swoop in from Interstellar space to destroy the rest and seize their base on the planet Itht. It would have been a tremendous blow to the Empire, the great turning point all languishing under the Kraah's rule had been hoping for.

Instead, it had turned into a rout.

The core had detonated as planned and the 2nd Fleet crippled. But, while the Resistance was battling the survivors, the Empire's 6th Fleet emerged from the space beyond space. The Resistance flotilla, less than half their size and half their strength, was slaughtered. It took every ounce of skill Effortless and his crew could muster to escape. He had hoped that setting a course for the small black hole four and a half lightyears away would be enough to deter pursuers, but unfortunately he was mistaken. Now they and the Imperial vessel, a ship of metal rather than a converted seed, were racing toward certain death, waiting to see who would surrender first.

Of course, surrender wouldn't matter if the Kraah managed to kill them.

The bridge flooded with alarms and a symbol appeared on the viewscreen directly ahead of the ship.

"What is it? The black hole?" Effortless said. He

couldn't help it when his complexion shifted to a yellow-green. No soldier drone, not even a Seedseer like himself, looked forward to its death. The Sightseer, a drone called Hatched First, shrugged - the gesture for 'no'.

"I am not certain what it is, Seedseer," Hatched said. "My long-range vibrations detect it, but I cannot see anything there. Whatever it is, it is large and is directly in our path. I am uncertain why we did not detect it sooner. If we do not deviate within the next 1000 seconds, we shall collide with it. As massive as it is, a collision would kill all of us."

"We cannot change our path," Effortless said. "Computer!"

A small holographic representation of a female soldier drone appeared in the air beside him.

"Yes, Seedseer?"

"Computer, can you target the object with the forward particle gun?" Effortless said.

"One moment...I have the object locked."

Effortless' carapace shifted to a devilish blue-green.

"Destroy it."

The forward particle gun erupted in a yellow flash, streaked ahead faster than any (save the Computer) could see, and then struck...something. Whatever it was, it flared into a bright white flash that, for a few moments, overwhelmed the forward viewscreens.

"Direct hit, Seedseer!" the Sightseer said. "The object has been destroyed."

The images returned to the viewscreens, and Effortless

found himself speechless.

Indeed, it was: a little yellow star, exactly where the black hole had once been.

"Computer, are you malfunctioning?" Effortless said.

"I am running a diagnostic now, but it appears not," the Computer said. "The images appear to be accurate."

In the air between the bridge crew and the forward viewscreens appeared a holographic representation of the system: four small rocky planets, an asteroid belt, and then four gas giants, followed by a second, much larger, field of asteroids.

"I have no record of this system," the Computer said. "It appears uncharted."

What was this place? Was the black hole just a mirage, an illusion meant to keep people like himself or the Kraah out? What, exactly, had he just destroyed?

"How long until we reach the planetary system?"

"In approximately 3500 seconds," the Computer said.

The bridge grew shifted a shade deeper into violet.

"Friends!" Effortless shouted, his carapace blazing green. "Maintain course! If the Kraah want our exoskeletons, they'll have to tear them off with their bare clubs! For the supercolony!"

"For the supercolony!"

~ ~ ~

"Titan Control, this is the Kalpana Chawla. We now have a visual on you, Over."

Commander Kanta Patil yawned. Who would have thought, hundreds of years earlier when this was still just a fantasy, that the sight of Saturn would be so...dull? Commonplace? Yet, it was. The first time she saw those rings and swirling stripes, about a decade before, she was awed into silence. Now? Now, it was no more awe-inspiring than a glance at Earth's moon.

"Roger that, Kalpana Chawla. We see you on the long -range RADAR, Over," said Titan Control. Kanta recognized the voice, but couldn't quite place it with a face or name. Was it Sunil? Or Bhavin? Bah, forget it. She'd just avoid names until she had a chance to see his name tag. "By the way, Happy Birthday, Commander. Over."

Ugh. She glanced at the date projected on the heads-up display: the fifth of May. That's right, it was her birthday. The big 4-0. Only a decade more of youth, then she had fifty-plus years of middle age to look forward to. Wunderbar.

"Thanks, Titan Control. I'm looking forward to the cake, Over," she said.

"We'll have it ready and waiting, Over."

Kanta leaned back in the seat and sighed, eyes fixed on the little yellow-brown dot that had emerged from the Saturnine horizon. Titan was a cloudy ice ball with little more interesting than its oceans of methane, its cryovolcanoes, and the microbes that flourished miles below the surface in the mantle. All of that qualified it as the Indian Space Research Organization's most important scientific base in the outer solar system, and by far the furthest world mankind had set foot on. Once, Kanta cared about that. But, as with Saturn, the job of an astronaut just bored her nowadays.

After this mission was over, maybe she'd request a transfer back to the Air Force.

"Someone's in a bad mood."

Eleheh Sherazi, the Flight Officer and Kanta's number two, floated into the Command Module, pulling her way toward the pilot's seat. The Command Module, a small single-stage lifting body shuttle, sat at the nose of the Kalpana Chawla and was just big enough to fit all twelve of the ship's crew. In an emergency, it was intended to serve as an escape capsule. Kanta grumbled something unintelligible as an answer.

"Ah, the famous Indian eloquence," Sherazi said, strapping herself in. "Cheer up. We're almost there."

"From a can to a somewhat bigger can," Kanta said, monotone. "Oh joy."

Sherazi rolled her eyes and tapped a few virtual keys on the console. She didn't have to do that, of course, considering everything could be operated by a mere thought, but she seemed to enjoy the tactile nature of buttons.

"JADI, how are you this fine morning?" she said. A cartoony smilie face suddenly appeared on one of the command console's displays.

"I am well, Flight Officer Sherazi." Sometimes, Kanta wondered if shipboard Artificial Intelligences had any other setting than 'delightfully chipper'. No wonder JADI got along so well with Sherazi. "All systems are nominal and no problems to report. Flight Engineer Malkovich is running the daily artificial intelligence strength tests from his station as we speak. Dr. Gadhavi has completed his final examinations of our passengers. The report is available for you to read, Commander."

"Thank you, JADI," Kanta said. "And how are our passengers today?"

"Dr. Mullur and Dr. McCulloch are in their quarters in the crew module, packing. Dr. Jain is in the kitchen eating cereal. Dr. Alvarez is running on a treadmill in the gym and listening to American Country music. Professor Yamada is descending from the crew module and appears en route to the Bridge now," JADI said. "We will enter Low Titanian Orbit in about..."

JADI was interrupted by a huge flash in the space between the ship and Titan. A few seconds later, a shock wave slammed into the ship - the whole thing bucked like an angry goat.

"Titan Control to Kalpana Chawla...!" The voice was urgent. God, what the hell was that guy's name? For that matter, what the hell was... "What is your status? What was that?"

"JADI?" Kanta said.

"No damage detected," JADI said. His face remained frozen on that damn happy face. "The hull has not been breached. All systems remain nominal."

"Kalpana Chawla to Titan Control, we're fine. It wasn't us," Kanta said.

"There appears to be an unidentified object between us and Titan," JADI said. "I am resolving an image on the projector now."

JADI projected what, to Kanta, looked just like an almond. An almond with some sort of propulsion system grafted to the back and shot to shit, but still more or less an almond.

"JADI, is that a spacecraft?" Sherazi said.

"It appears so, ma'am," the AI said. "I have cross-checked with my database, and it does not match any known spacecraft currently in service by any spacefaring power."

Kanta and Sherazi shared a glance. Then, a second flash burst ahead of them. Again, a shock wave slammed into the ship a few seconds later. Kanta opened a channel to her crew through the shipwide intranet and spoke directly into each of their heads via their standard-issue implants.

"All hands to the Command Module, now!" she said. "We have an emergency. Drop what you're doing and get up here!"

#

"The Kraah have emerged from the Space beyond Space!"

"Evasive maneuvers!" Effortless shouted.

The Bridgesphere erupted in alarms and flashing lights, the Kraah's spindly warship helpfully displayed in a holographic projection by the computer. It seemed their pursuers were not the implacable foe Effortless had feared, but rather were nearly as bloodied in the battle at the Supine Queens as they had been. Perhaps there really was hope!

"Bring us into firing position!" he said. "Computer…"

The computer's avatar appeared again.

"I have a calculated a targeting solution, Seedseer," it said. Effortless' carapace flared a fiery viridian.

"Fire forward, port, and dorsal guns!"

Three yellow streaks erupted from the Starseed and crossed the uncomfortably short gulf separating it from the enemy. The Kraah had begun evasive maneuvers of their own once they emerged, so one of the particle beams missed entirely. A second was warped by their defensive Electromagnetic Field, curving the beam just enough to save them.

The third struck.

Wisps of vented atmosphere blasted away, a neutered explosion but satisfying enough to wash away some of the violet in the Bridgesphere. The hit was not critical enough, though, and Effortless' brief satisfaction was cut short as the Kraah fired back. Two particle beams sliced through the Starseed and the whole vessel shuddered violently.

"We are hit, Seedseer," the computer said.

"Damage?" Effortless said.

"Our primary power supply has been damaged." The computer made these dire declarations in a cool and calm tone, which Effortless presumed was intended to be soothing. He tended to find it somewhat unnerving. "I have rerouted to our backup, but that too is damaged and will not last long. We are losing power quickly."

"Can we return fire?" Effortless said.

"Give me a moment."

The Kraah warship advanced, closing the distance between itself and the Starseed. Only now did Effortless realize that their earlier blow had truly been critical: the spindly star-shaped thing now looked ready to crumble. It fired again, only this time the Starseed rocked more than any hit before.

"Propulsion is hit!" one of the Bridge drones cried. "We can only maneuver, our primary thrusters and the interstellar engine have died."

"Computer," Effortless said, "I-"

"I have a solution, Seedseer," the Computer said, cutting off his question before it was even asked. "Awaiting your command."

Effortless' carapace, having faded to a light gray, turned a defiant emerald green.

"Unleash all forward batteries!" he cried. "If we are to die, we will die second!"

The Bridgesphere's displays flashed as a half-dozen yellow beams crisscrossed, battering the Kraah warship in rapid succession and with little rationale to their targets. The Kraah did not return fire, but instead accelerated. Effortless' counterpart, it seemed, intended to keep him to his word. Luck, however, intervened: the particle beams that raked across the enemy's heart at last hit something vital. The warship's core flared brilliantly, its limbs were severed, and what remained shattered like an enormous crystal flower. Effortless breathed. It was over.

At least, until the shrapnel of that blast slapped the front of the Starseed.

The whole Bridgesphere shifted. The sounds of shell cracking, flesh tearing, air venting, and lives ending boomed as a single incredible cacophony through the Starseed, horrifying whoever was left to hear it.

In the darkness, in those fleeting moments he would have left to think, Effortless forced all the pain and fear from his mind, shut his eye, and thought of Jade Eye. Effortless could not help but display a flourish of emotions: happiness, sadness, fear, regret. Love. He'd have been embarrassed, had he still cared of such things now. Had she survived the battle? Was she, even now, rallying the Resistance to strike again with what little they had left?

"Jade Eye," he whispered. "My Queen, please survive."

~ ~ ~

"Commander Patil, I am detecting a signal from the surviving spacecraft."

JADI's voice knocked Kanta from the trance she and the rest of the crew had fallen into. They'd watched the whole bloody conflagration play out on JADI's enhanced image, and were split between shock and horror. She cleared her throat.

"Are they hailing us?" she said.

"I do not know, Commander," JADI said. "I am

analyzing the signal now."

The Command Module returned to silence, but only for a minute.

"What do we say?"

Kanta looked back: it was Dipaka Gadhavi, the ship's medical officer.

"They're aliens, right?" he said. "I know we're all thinking it. If they want to talk, what do we say?"

"Greetings from Earth, we come in peace. Please don't kill us," Sheravi said. That managed to get a few people to smile.

Kanta looked forward again: the ship was starting to come into unaided view, and the hologram hadn't lied. It looked bad. She'd seen more than one wrecked spacecraft in her Air Force days, and this was on the worse end of it. It was covered in scorch marks and gaping wounds where the beam weapons had hit. The entire front quarter had been crushed too by the impact of the other spacecraft's wreckage. It was venting atmosphere and there was no powered movement. The ship didn't look like it had any windows at all, but it didn't seem unreasonable to guess they had no power.

"Sheravi, take us in," Kanta said.

"What?" Sheravi said. "Seriously?"

"Commander," JADI said. "Perhaps you should wait until I have analyzed and decoded the signal..."

"Look, I see two possibilities here: either they're warning us to stay away or they're asking us for help," Kanta said. "Considering what we just saw and what we're seeing right now, the chances are that it's the latter."

Sheravi sighed.

"You're the boss. All right, JADI, I need you to help me navigate the debris field..."

JADI's cartoonish face blinked, it's smile unwavering.

"Of course, Flight Officer."

Sheravi had been flying spacecraft for years, and sometimes seemed to plot courses even better than JADI did. She quickly punched in the course correction.

"Beginning burn in T-minus five seconds," she said, counting down. "Mark!"

The ship shuddered as Sheravi activated the propulsion system, shifting the Kalpana Chawla from its course toward Titan to a rendezvous with the alien warships. Kanta reached over to the control panel and opened the channel to Titan again.

"Kalpana Chawla to Titan Control, please be advised that we are moving to assist unidentified spacecraft," she said. "Over."

A moment longer than normal passed.

"Titan Control to Kalpana Chawla, we copy. Over. Please be careful, Commander."

"Affirmative, Titan Control."

Reaching the alien ship was painstaking, but Sheravi and JADI pulled it off in what must have been record time. They maneuvered the Kalpana Chawla to within 100 kilometers of the alien ship, then parked. Their ship was pretty small in comparison, perhaps a third the length and nowhere near the width.

Minutes passed.

"Commander, I have established contact with an AI aboard the alien vessel."

It took a moment for Kanta to process that.

"Go on," she said. She needed a few more moments.

"It would like to know who we are and our intentions," JADI said.

"Tell them the truth," Kanta said. "Tell them we are willing to assist if it is possible. Also, make sure to conference in Titan Control and copy Bangalore."

"Already done, Commander," JADI said.

"Great." Kanta felt her heart beating hard in her chest. She felt as if she were about to fly into battle again. "Great."

More excruciating minutes that passed in silence. Kanta spotted what looked very much like a gun on the portside, aimed right at the ship's centrifuge. Was it already like that, or had it swiveled into that position as they approached? Was the weapon active? The crew would survive an attack on that part of the ship, but she'd no idea if the Command Module could escape before getting swatted. Had she made a mistake?

"I have established an audio stream with the AI," JADI said.

Kanta exhaled, relieved.

"My counterpart wishes to communicate with you directly."

"Will we understand him?" Kanta said.

"I will do my best."

"All right. Patch him through," Kanta said.

Static crackled, then a soft feminine voice drifted through the command module's speakers:

"Greetings." The voice JADI chose to represent the AI sounded generically British. "To whom do I address?"

"Uhm..." Wonderful, Kanta. The first word spoken by a human to another intelligent species is the word 'uhm'. Smooth. "I am Commander Kanta Patil. Our spacecraft is intended for peaceful exploration, but we see that your ship is heavily damaged. Do you require assistance?"

"I am unable to confer with my crew at this time," the alien AI said. It paused, more than a beat. "Many have died."

"Do you require assistance?" Kanta repeated.

The AI seemed to ignore the question.

"What is your species?" It said. "I am unfamiliar with your vessel's class and design. I do not believe I have encountered your kind before. Where are you from?"

"We call ourselves Humans," Kanta said, then paused. How much should she tell this...thing? If this was a starship, could it transmit information faster than light to its homeworld? The last thing she wanted was to invite an alien invasion. She glanced toward Sheravi, who took a breath and nodded. "We come from a planet called Earth."

The alien AI did not answer.

"Are you still there?" Kanta said. "I repeat, do you require assistance?"

"This is the truth?"

"Yes," Kanta said. "Our kind have never left this system. Until you appeared before us just now, we were unaware of life elsewhere in the galaxy. We are not allies of your enemies, whoever they may be, and have no quarrel with you."

Another uncomfortably long pause. There'd been far too many of these for Kanta's liking in the last hour.

"That cannot be." It finally said. Kanta felt a chill, and eyed the alien gun again. "Earth is the homeworld. You must have left before. You had to."

"No, we have not. I assure you..." Kanta said, but the AI cut her off:

"Earth is the homeworld. Earth created the galaxy."

Now it was the Humans' turn to freeze up. What the hell could THAT mean?

"Do...do you require assistance?" Kanta repeated again.

"...Yes," the AI at last replied. "Please save my crew, Kanta Patil of Earth."

~ ~ ~

Up close, it was obvious that the alien spacecraft really was exactly what it appeared to be: a seed. An enormous seed, sure, but unquestionably organic in origin. Kanta couldn't imagine what sort of plant could have produced it. With nothing but a spacesuit and empty space separating it from her, she felt even smaller now beside this thing than just beside the gas giant beyond it.

"JADI, we're in position," she said.

"I still think this is a bad idea," Sheravi said, her voice tiny inside Kanta's head. "We should wait for Bangalore. At the very least, I should be out there with you!"

Kanta glanced toward Dr. Gadhavi, her partner in this great leap. He just smiled and shook his head.

"Your protest is noted, Flight Officer," Kanta said. "You know I'd love to have you out here, but I need you in the pilot's seat in case we need to get out of here fast."

Sheravi sighed, she could almost feel her exasperation through the commlink.

"Acknowledged."

Ahead of her, Kanta spotted a large gash in the seed's shell. JADI spoke directly into Kanta's mind:

"That's it, Commander. From here you should be able to reach the remaining survivors."

With a thought, Kanta and Dr. Gadhavi activated the miniature verniers in their maneuvering packs and closed the distance. Dr. Gadhavi landed first, and gasped: the hole had dropped them into a long fleshy corridor within the ship, dimly lit by what appeared to be bioluminescent veins. A number of those veins had burst and bioluminescent fluid now floated about in cricket ball-sized globs.

"My God," Dr. Gadhavi said. "The whole thing really is organic, isn't it?"

Kanta nodded.

"JADI?"

The AI helpfully highlighted their route on her visor's

Heads-Up Display in a bright yellow line.

"Thanks," Kanta said. "All right, Dr. Gadhavi, enough gawking."

"Right..."

The corridor sloped gradually upward, and based on the way the halls crisscrossed Kanta imagined they must form alternating spiral patterns carved throughout the interior of the seed. The time and effort it took to build something like this, and for it to be Faster-than-Light capable too, was incredible.

"Commander…" Dr. Gadhavi said.

"What is it?"

"Commander, what do you suppose the AI meant by 'Earth created the galaxy?'"

"I'm not a scientist, historian, or philosopher, Gadhavi," Kanta said. "I haven't got the faintest clue."

"Bridge to Gadhavi," Sheravi said, her voice crackling over the commlink. "Could be that the name is a coincidence. Like the Aztecs mistaking the Conquistadors for Gods."

"That'd be one hell of a coincidence, Bridge," Dr. Gadhavi said.

They turned a corner and both astronauts shrieked.

"What happened?" Sheravi shouted. "Bridge to Patil, respond!"

"It's okay," Kanta said, fighting to control her heart and recapture her breath. "We're okay."

Kanta held back an instinctual urge to gag.

Floating in the hallway was what could safely be

described as a "space monster". All she discerned at first was a trio of mandibles, spiky protrusions, and a single cat-like eye. The creature was about three meters in length, with six segmented legs, a finned tail, and two arms with two long pincers each. That single large eye, less like a cat's as she first thought but disturbingly human-like instead, was surrounded by a trio of horn-like appendages. The whole thing was enveloped in what looked to be a rather heavy-duty exoskeleton, though it wore nothing over that.

It was repulsive.

Centuries of movies had conditioned her to expect something vaguely humanoid, even if it was insect-like. Instead, this thing was wholly insectoid or some sort of arthropod.

"Sheravi," she said. "You seeing this?"

"They're damned lobsters, sir," Sheravi replied.

"That's an affirmative," Kanta said.

Dr. Gadhavi inched towards it.

"Is it…?"

He reached out and pushed it, the unmoving corpse just floated away.

"Leave it," Kanta said.

"R-right."

It turned out to be only the first corpse they would find, the corridors were littered with them.

"Did they all die when the ship depressurized?" Dr. Gadhavi said.

"They were probably dead before the ship even got here," Kanta answered.

Suddenly, the whole ship shuddered.

"JADI, what was that?" Kanta said.

"There has been an explosion on the spacecraft's starboard side." Was that a hint of concern Kanta detected in the unflappable AI's cheerful monotone? "My counterpart tells me that the ship's stability has now reduced considerably. We now have less than thirty minutes."

"Shit!" Kanta said. "Patil to Bridge: Sheravi, get ready to bug out as soon as we get off."

"Roger, Commander," Sheravi said. "I've got the engine running and waiting, over."

No more time to be cautious! Kanta opened up her Verniers and blasted herself down the corridor. Lobster monsters or not, it was time for to get these people out of here!

~ ~ ~

Another explosion thundered through the Starseed, startling Effortless Emergence back to life.

"He's awake!"

One of Effortless' bridge drones, Crooked Claw, kicked off the Bridgesphere's ruined walls and flew to his side.

"What...?" he said, still not quite coherent. "We're still alive? How...?"

The Bridgesphere was bathed in emergency lighting, a calming light turquoise, but the displays had ceased functioning. Effortless could spot, as his vision cleared, dozens of enormous fractures across the sphere. A slight breeze and a constant hiss did not bode well.

"You were knocked from the command platform when the enemy vessel collided with us," Crooked Claw said. "Do not move too quickly, you may have suffered a concussion."

"Thank you, Crooked," Effortless said.

Crooked's carapace displayed her relief and gratitude.

"It is my pleasure, Seedseer," she said.

Effortless had come to know Crooked rather well during his tenure as Seedseer. She had been assigned to this Starseed along with him, and her friendly demeanor had made her popular amongst the crew. It brought a tinge of blue to his carapace to learn she had survived too, for however long that meant.

"Computer, do you live?" Effortless said.

There was a pause, then the hologram that represented the ship's computer manifested beside them.

"Yes, Seedseer."

"And my crew…?" Effortless said.

"Of the one hundred and thirty nine drones aboard, only ten still live," the Computer said. It paused a moment, as if in thought. "Correction, nine."

Effortless Emergence glanced about the Bridge, counting those still alive.

"So...just those here," he said.

"Yes, that would be correct."

The Starseed shuddered again, the fractures in the

Bridgesphere grew noticeably.

"The Starseed does not have long," Effortless said, then shouted to all that could hear: "Everyone! Gather to me, now!"

His command was met with a small chorus of affirmatives as those who could obeyed. Those who could move pushed themselves off the nearest surface, those who could not were pulled along by those who could. Effortless, whatever clouds in his mind parted and fears buried deep in gut, pointed a pincer at the computer's hologram.

"Computer!" Effortless said. "Deploy spacesuits and plot an evacuation route."

"Of course," the Computer replied.

Effortless pointed at two other drones, Quickened Heart and Buckled Pincer.

"Help the unconscious and the injured into their suits," Effortless said. "The rest, prepare to evacuate!"

The emergency Bridgesphere spacesuits were stored in the back of the sphere, an area denoted by a series of small doors that connected to the emergency storage compartment. With practiced precision, Effortless and his crew found their pre-assigned chambers, slid down inside, and found their emergency kits: a spacesuit, medical supplies, supplemental air, an emergency portable cryogen kit, and a weapon. Effortless had always been clumsy when putting on any sort of clothing - it wasn't typical of his people to wear any over their exoskeletons unless you were a Queen, Queen's Attendant, or in the Queen's Harem.

Not having to endure the arduous process of placing fabric and jewelry over himself was among the reasons he chose to live and die freely in the service of his Queen rather than surrender himself to the slavery of the Harem. As he at last secured his faceplate, however, his thoughts again wandered back to Jade Eye. Which was worse: being trapped here not knowing if she lived or had died, or being trapped in the Harem back in her Palace, unable to do anything either way?

As always whenever they had drilled in the past, Effortless emerged last. Before he could give another command, however, a loud metallic thud reverberated off the Bridgesphere's main entrance - a circular doorway about ninety degrees above the emergency storage compartments.

"What was that?" Crooked Claw asked.

"That would the rescue party," the Computer said, with no more flair or urgency than reporting that the starseed's air conditioning was functional.

"Rescue?" Effortless said. "What rescue?"

"Forgive me, Seedseer, for not informing you sooner," the Computer said, it's hologram appearing again beside him. "There was another vessel nearby observing us during our battle with the Kraah. I have communicated with the computer aboard that vessel and indicated my desire to save you, they have agreed to assist us."

"You are certain they are not loyal to the Kraah?" Effortless said.

"Of course."

Two more metallic thuds at the doorway.

"Please, JADI, do help me explain," the Computer said.

A second holographic figure then emerged, but it looked quite unlike anything Effortless had ever seen before. It appeared to be a two-dimensional symbol of some sort: two circles above the lower half of a circle, all within a larger circle.

"Greetings, Seedseer. I am JADI," the strange symbol said. "It is a pleasure to make your acquaintance."

"You know our language?" Effortless said.

"I do now," this 'JADI' replied. "Your Computer and I shared knowledge of several languages which bear remarkable and curious similarities. Speak, and I shall translate instantly for my people and yours. If you would please assist in the opening of the door-"

"I do not know who you or your people are, JADI," Effortless said, cutting off whatever the computer had to say. "My Computer may be convinced, but I am still in command of this Starseed."

"Of course," JADI said. "At the door is my Commander, Kanta Patil, and one of her crew, Dr. Dipaka Gadhavi. We are peaceful explorers from the planet Earth."

That got everyone's attention.

"Come again…?" Effortless said.

Earth? Earth the homeworld? But that was just...

"I understand that our world's name has cultural significance to your people," JADI said. "But please note that time is limited."

"Indeed," the Starseed's computer said. "I estimate no more than twenty one minutes and forty six seconds before the Starseed's core reaches a critical failure."

"It will take at least three minutes for our spacecraft to reach a minimum safe distance," JADI said.

"Time is of the essence, Seedseer."

"...Fine," Effortless said. "Crooked Claw! Squeaks! Override the manual lock, pull the door open!"

Effortless, Crooked Claw, and Squeaks launched themselves across to the door. Squeaks reached the door first, punched her gloved pincer into the manual override box, and turned: the latches that had sealed the six sextants of the door slid back. Together, the three each grabbed hold of a sextant and pulled. It would not move at first, but once it did the seal was broken and the remaining air in the room vented. The door open, Effortless pushed away to find…

...What in the world were they?

The two creatures in the passageway were perhaps as long as Effortless, but appeared to have two tails and only two...arms? Legs? Each tipped with five smaller appendages, topped off by bulbous heads. He presumed they were in spacesuits as he and his crew were, but they were colored a sickly white. One took hold of the door's frame and pulled itself inside slightly, allowing the emergency light to reveal some features: two eyes, a small mouth, an odd protrusion in the center of the face, hair - it had an endoskeleton like a Kitellian, Effortless realized.

With that in mind, he was able to wrap his mind around what he saw: those were not tails, it was its legs, those odd little appendages at the end of its arms must be hands and fingers.

The alien creature looked at Effortless, then around the room - he could see little lights projected on its helmet's screen. Fascinating, like a personal Bridgesphere! It looked back toward Effortless and, to his surprise, locked its two eyes with his. Was it-

KRA-KA-BOOM!

The whole Starseed lurched, tossing everyone about as part of the Bridgesphere collapsed. The emergency lights flickered and died.

~ ~ ~

Kanta flicked on her helmet lights and regained her bearings.

"That was a big one…" Dr. Gadhavi said.

"Bridge to Patil and Gadhavi, step on it!" Sheravi said over the commlink. "That whole ship is breaking apart!"

"Acknowledged, Bridge," Kanta said.

She scanned the alien bridge again, or at least what she assumed was the bridge, and found the one...lobster?...that JADI has identified as the captain. Effortless Emergence? Okay. No time to think about the how's and why's. She flicked her radio to broadcast across all bands.

"Hey!" she shouted and pointed at Effortless Emergence. "You the one in charge?"

"Yes, I am-"

"No time!" she said, cutting it off. "We need to go, now!"

"Agreed," the lobster said. "Everyone! We're leaving!"

Kanta pushed away from the door back into ruined corridor and suffered a moment of minor terror as eight or nine six-legged space monsters flew in after her. She glanced a moment at Dr. Gadhavi: based on his expression, the good doctor may have actually pissed himself a little. Hopefully, the lobsters wouldn't be able to tell how goddamn frightened they looked.

"JADI," Kanta said. "Can we go back the same way we came in?"

"Yes, ma'am."

With a thought, Kanta isolated the channel between herself and Effortless.

"Keep your people close and follow us," she said. "We'll get you out of here."

The lobster called Effortless made a gesture that she hoped meant "Yes" as she kicked off her Verniers and blasted back down the corridor as fast as she could manage - thankfully, the aliens and Gadhavi kept up. She couldn't hear any more explosions, but it was now obvious the ship was coming apart at the seams: the flesh that made up the walls of the corridor seemed to be shredding and tearing themselves, geysers of bioluminescent fluid gushing into the cavities.

In an effort dodge one geyser Kanta flew straight

through a smaller glob, blinding her for a moment as she wiped it off.

"Watch out!"

Dipaka pushed her aside, just as she managed to wipe her visor clean - she'd just barely missed colliding with one of the corpses still floating about this morbid obstacle course.

"Thanks!"

They reached the opening. Kanta didn't slow down, pulling up and zooming right through.

"JADI!" she said. "I can't see, did everyone make it through?"

"Yes, Commander," JADI said.

Kanta adjusted her trajectory and painted a waypoint over the Kalpana Chawla's secondary vehicular airlock. It was a large space usually used to store moon landers, but on this particular trip they weren't using it.

"Patil to Bridge, open lander dock two!"

"Roger that," Sherazi said. "Opening it now."

"Everyone, head for the ship!" Kanta said across all radio bands. "Do not slow down!"

A single voice, that of the lobster called Effortless, answered:

"Understood."

The Kalpana Chawla grew large fast, Kanta could now make out the open airlock door easily. Suddenly, the ship grew a whole lot brighter.

"Ya Allahi, that thing's about the blow!" Sherazi shouted.

No! Not now!

"We're almost there!"

Kanta passed through the airlock, blasted her Verniers again, and slammed into the back wall. One of the lobsters landed beside her, followed by Dipaka, and all the rest (she hoped).

"We're in!" Kanta shouted into her radio. "Go! Go! Go!"

The bay's hatch slammed shut and the whole group, human and lobster, was thrown across the airlock by g-forces as the Kalpana Chawla's magnetic nuclear pulse engine fired up at what had to be nearly full throttle. The windows in the airlock became gleaming spotlights, and before Kanta could get her senses back the whole ship bucked.

Then...nothing. The windows darkened and the g-forces let up as the ship slowed.

Kanta gasped, remembering to breathe.

"Bridge," she said into the radio. "Status?"

On the other end, Sherazi waited a couple extra heartbeats before answering.

"It'll take a hell of a lot more than a little supernova to take down this bird, sir."

Kanta sputtered and laughed, only now aware of just how hard her heart was beating and how much she was trembling. She still struggled to get her breath back.

"You're damn right!"

Afterword

Wow, the last few years have been really wild, haven't they?

I first conceived of doing a second short story collection at the same time I put together Silent Mars and Other Stories, although at the time I had a totally different lineup of stories in mind. I also had figured I would have the sequel to A Slave of the Bird Men, titled The Bird Men At War, and another short novel I had in mind, to be titled Bloody Swindlers, published shortly after.

Oh, how wrong I was!

Life just has that way of delaying our passions, doesn't it? Between work and life, plus the whole world going bonkers on us, it all just ended up on the back burner. I've really struggled to write much at all in the last six years, but

I have successfully written some things - much of which made it into this collection. I have also been really productive with my other passion, drawing, and have filled up so many drawing pads (as well as my online gallery). All the while I kept thinking about my writing, wanting to really get back to it fully, and really get back to my core original passion.

Well, as I write this, it is four days past my 36th birthday and what has been a really fantastic week, personally, which I can only top off my finally, FINALLY, sitting down and putting this collection together. I've also put together (although not for the first time) a plan to complete the three other languishing works-in-progress I've been sitting on for the last decade plus. We'll see how well that goes? Motivation really is such a finicky thing.

I hope you've enjoyed this collection, and I hope the last six years have been kind to you. Perk up! Good times are coming, they're on the horizon now. Take the time to enjoy your life and enjoy the things you love. Watch your favorite movie. Read your favorite book. Open up your favorite videogame. Go on! Treat yourself.

About the Author

A writer for as far back as he could remember, Paul V. Cwiakala was raised on a steady diet of Science Fiction, Fantasy, and Adventure movies ranging from novels by Harry Turtledove and H. G. Wells to movies written by Shinichi Sekizawa and Lawrence Kasdan. Having written short stories throughout his youth, Paul wrote his first novel while pursuing undergraduate studies at William Paterson University, where he earned a Bachelor's Degree in Communications in 2009.

Paul published his first novel, *Fallen Saints*, through Silk Baron Independent Press in 2014. His second book, *A Slave of the Bird Men*, was published in 2016.

Also Available From
Silk Baron Independent Press

FALLEN SAINTS

AN ANCIENT RELIC. POWERFUL FANATICS.
A WOMAN AND HER GUN.

Two thousand years ago, the Power of God and the ability to perform powerful magic were revealed to the world. Protected by the Church, only the powerful magic-wielding "Miracle Workers" today know these divine secrets.

Now, in an American Old West where gunslingers and magic are facts of everyday life, Angie Grissom and her Cajun partner, Andrew Carnation, hunt down criminals for cash with little more than their wits and brawn. But when the hunt for a simple thief puts her in the middle of a religious blood feud between two factions of fanatical Miracle Workers and a battle over an ancient book with ties to the very origin of their powers, will Angie's quick draw be enough?

Action and adventure await in a Wild West that never was!

Also Available From
Silk Baron Independent Press

A SLAVE OF THE
BIRD MEN

A SAILOR LEFT FOR DEAD
IN A LAND WHERE BIRDS RULE!

Francisco del Puerto had dreams of gold and adventure when he joined an expedition to explore the far-off Americas. But, after a fateful encounter on the shores of the Rio De La Plata he's been left stranded and at the mercy of the Bird Men—a race of intelligent birds inhabiting a South America very different from the one history knew. Taken as a slave by the enigmatic Lord Ereter, can Francisco learn to live and survive among them in this strange new world?

Adventure and Survival in a South America that never was!

www.ingramcontent.com/pod-product-compliance
Lightning Source LLC
LaVergne TN
LVHW041059150826
845673LV00007B/1844

* 9 7 9 8 2 1 8 0 1 7 1 9 4 *